BEHIND CLOSED DOORS

Crossing the room, I noticed one door of the closet slightly ajar and swung my left arm out absently to close it.

The door swung violently back, hitting the end of my middle finger so hard I heard the bone crack. I screamed at the top of my lungs. Somebody lunged out of the closet and knocked me down, going flat out for the door.

My right had found something that moved, a stool or a small chair. From the floor, I threw it as hard as I could at the figure running away. It thudded into his back, driving him forward so he smacked into the door across the hall. He turned, blood streaming down the front of his face, his right hand groping at his back. I had my feet under me and was getting up, but the right hand came away from his back, holding a gun....

TRIPLE PLAY

• A JAKE HINES MYSTERY •

ELIZABETH GUNN

A DELL BOOK

Published by
Dell Publishing
a division of
Bantam Doubleday Dell Publishing Group, Inc.
1540 Broadway
New York, New York 10036

ALL THE SITUATIONS and characters in this book are fictitious, but I
would like to thank John Sibley, Deputy Chief of Police of Rochester,
Minnesota, who gave me kind and patient help with matters of terminolo-
gy and procedure in the law enforcement community.

ISBN: 0-440-22635-X

Reprinted by arrangement with Walker Publishing Company, Inc.

Printed in the United States of America

Published simultaneously in Canada

December 1998

10   9   8   7   6   5   4   3   2   1

WCD

To Phil Gunn,
who makes everything possible

· ONE ·

"Come on," I said, "let's do it now."

"In the yard, are you crazy?" Nancy laughed and turned away. I reached out for her, but she skittered across the lawn, staying just ahead of me, teasing. I followed her, panting hilariously, stretching out my arms and pushing to gain speed, straining to catch her. Her hair shone glossy in the dappled sunlight, and her laughter rang like bells. Another bell rang somewhere, too; I ran faster, but the noise grew louder and she faded as the telephone pierced my dream. I groped for it through a haze of desire.

"Jake? Ed Gray." The lieutenant's good at waking people; he takes his time. After a couple of seconds he asked, a little firmer, "Jake? You awake?"

"Glah," I said, more or less. I turned on the light and

squinted at the clock on my night stand. Five past two. In the morning? Of curse, in the morning, ding-dong. I sat up and rejoined the force. "What is it, Ed?"

"Uh, kinda serious business, I guess," Ed said, resuming his usual commanding baritone. "Vince Greeley says he's got a DOA, which according to him it's gotta be a homicide. Seems like the victim is pretty messed up . . . Vince claims he's never seen anything like it." I heard his console rattle, and a loud, angry voice shouting drunkenly in the near distance. "I thought you better have a look before I called the coroner."

"The cor—Ed, are you sure we need the coroner? Where is Vince?"

"In the park. Pioneer Park. Where the softball diamonds are, in the northwest corner behind the pool. Harley Mundt's his partner, he's there too. They were doing routine drive-bys in section thirteen, and they saw the side gate of the park standing open. They went in to check and found this dead guy in there. Right smack dab on home plate, Vince says, on playing field two. Hold on a minute."

Two dead little *thunks* sounded on the line as he shunted his other calls out to the duty sergeant. As soon as the buzzing stopped, he barked a sharp order that got somebody to slam a door on the shouting drunk. He sucked air in the sudden silence, blew it out, and finished, softly, "You better go see this, Jake. You wanna let me know about the coroner after you get over there?"

"I'll call him if I need him," I said. "Where'll I find Greeley and Mundt? At the side gate on Eleventh? Or—"

"No, no, the east side, Jake, on Webster. The gate's between Eighth and Ninth Streets, but you gotta go east on Ninth, remember; Eighth is one way going west out there. Take the Beltway; Broadway's still busy from the bars." I hung up quickly to escape his parking instructions. Lieutenant Gray's normal bossiness gets worse as the night goes along.

Five years in the detective division have not been wasted on me; I can get dressed fast. Chinos and a blazer satisfy the dress code, so that's what I mostly wear. And I'm a slave to habit: shirts in the middle drawer, ties on a hanger, shoes on a rack. The Glock is in its holster, on its own belt, always in the same spot on the closet shelf. In five minutes I was twisting the spring-loaded lock on my front door. I eased it shut till I heard it click and padded quietly down the front steps on rubber soles. People like having a cop living in their neighborhood, as long as his night calls don't wake them up.

Driving toward the Beltway, I punched up KQRS in Minneapolis, got Pearl Jam playing "Alive," adjusted the bass to just where I could see the ashtray vibrate, and drummed on the steering wheel to get my juices flowing. My body seemed to be waking up in sections. My hands and feet were behaving normally, but my nose was still cold, and the pit of my stomach felt as if I'd swallowed a coil of old rope. My brain was handling basic stuff like driving the car and humming off-key, but it was still coming up blank on the day of the week.

On the highway, I spotted the neon glare of an all-night convenience store, pulled in, and bought an enormous Styrofoam cup of black coffee. I slurped it anxiously, burning my lips, as I drove east toward Pioneer Park. Tuesday, I remembered suddenly; it was Monday night when I went to bed, so this has to be Tuesday morning. Thank you, Juan Valdez.

Turning off the highway into the quiet residential neighborhood leading to the park, I doused the radio, rolled my window down, and sucked in a big, delicious noseful of Minnesota in May. Lilacs, fresh-turned earth, sheep manure, and grass cuttings; heaven should only have it so good. Was last winter the longest and coldest on record, or do I ask that every year in May?

Anyway, Minnesota winters do make you really appreciate spring. Everybody in Rutherford says that, to explain to tourists why we live so far north in the temperate zone.

Strangers, meeting me for the first time, often ask me where I'm from. They think I'm an immigrant because my face looks wrong for the Upper Midwest, where most people are of Scandinavian, Irish, and German descent and have pale skin and blue eyes. My skin is cinnamon-colored, and I have, as a tactful teacher once put it, mixed features: straight black hair, almond-shaped dark brown eyes, dimples, and a nose like the late Shah of Iran's. Or Montezuma's, depending on how you look at it.

The jury is still out on who contributed what to my bloodlines, but I'm as native as it's possible to get: besides being born here, I was a ward of the state of Minnesota until I was eighteen years old. I grew up in Waseca. Also in Wabasha, Owatonna, Faribault, Winona, and Albert Lea. The foster home system keeps leftover kids from starving in snowbanks, but stability in caregivers is not one of its features. And to be fair, it's hard to place a kid who doesn't seem to fit any of the choices on the line marked "Race." Most of my caseworkers ended up checking the box after "Other."

I never met my parents, but I know who brought me into the world: the night janitor at the Red Wing Holiday Inn. He stepped outside to smoke a joint, one crisp October evening thirty-two years ago, heard what he thought was a kitten in the Dumpster, and dug me out of a mound of potato peelings. The night clerk called 911. By morning I was warmed up, and my paperwork was started. I was Case File #2975864 before I had my eyes open.

Given my unpromising beginnings, conventional wisdom might have predicted a career on the other side of law enforcement. And in fact, by junior high I was well on my way toward validating statistical probabilities, lightheartedly exploring the joys of truancy, pot smoking, and petty crime. But then a talented teacher in the Winona public school system noticed that math was easy for me and persuaded me to try studying.

"Trust me," he said, "it won't make your balls fall off to learn something. And it's fun."

Learning was not in vogue in my set; I had to smuggle the textbook home under my coat. At first I only did it to get his attention, but before long he'd shown me that information itself was a kick in the pants. By the end of the year he had me signed up for a summer math camp in the north woods, and I never went back to prowling cars. I turned into a math-and-science nerd, with just enough attitude to try for a scholarship at Rutherford Junior College. A thousand tests later, I got a shot at the Rutherford Police Department, and now I carry a badge that says I'm a good guy. Sometimes I have a guilty feeling that I picked up all the marbles when nobody was looking.

Expecting flashing dome lights, I almost missed Vince's unlighted squad car, parked in dense shade under a big oak. The little side gate stood open, a gap in the hedge-lined chain link fence that rings Pioneer Park. Harley Mundt was just visible, waiting in shadow inside the gate. No lights showed in the half-dozen houses that faced the park. Crickets clattered in the thick velvety darkness under the trees. I closed my car door gently and walked to the gate in silence.

"Hey, Jake," Harley growled softly through his big mustache. He pushed the gate closed as we shook hands. A thickset, meaty young guy, he'd only been on the Rutherford force a couple of years, most of the time on the night shift, where I seldom saw him. I remembered Vince told me he was good with tools, that he moonlighted in construction with his father and brothers. Never a big talker, he was definitely subdued right now.

"Vince is over there," Harley pointed through the shadows. Vince Greeley squatted in a pool of light that came in over the trees from the streetlamp outside. The park itself, since the last budget cutback, was unlighted after midnight. I crunched across gravel in the half-light, following a path between the fence and a small set of bleachers. In the gloom beyond Vince, I could dimly see dusty sandbags marking the bases of a softball diamond. Ruts marked the runners' paths between the bags. A scruffy grass outfield was off to the right beyond the bleachers; to the left, a chicken-wire backstop sagged from scarred uprights.

Vince straightened then and turned toward me, gleaming and elegant, looking like the poster cop as always. Meticulous about his appearance, he works out, gets his hair cut every three weeks, and keeps a steam iron and a shoeshine kit in his locker. The chief would like to keep him on days, where he's good for the department's image and keeps everybody else's socks pulled up. He's on nights this year so he can split daytime parenting chores with his wife while she finishes her RN course. If he's short on sleep, he keeps it to himself; Vince is too proud to act any way but cool.

Something lay on the ground in the gloom behind him. It was right on top of home plate, a pile of light-colored cushions and a big red—I felt a sudden surge of heat through my face and chest. My throat felt congested. The blood smell reached me, exotic and clinging. I made myself walk steadily forward to where Vince stood, balanced easily with his feet apart, the shadow of his peaked cap across his handsome face. Softly, so as not to wake the neighbors, I said, "Vince. What we got here?"

"Something goddamn odd, is what we got here, Jake." Vince's voice sounded dry. "Harley saw the gate open as we went by. I was driving. Game nights, you know, like last night, there's a park staffer detailed to stay late and lock up. They're pretty reliable, too. But tonight Harley said, 'Was that gate open like that when we went by at midnight?' and I said, 'Couldn't have been, we'da noticed it' . . ." He paused, thought a minute, and went on. "So we parked under the tree like that so's not to bother anybody, lotta older ladies live in this neighborhood alone, and they get pretty excited if they see a marked squad car here at night.

"We came in through the gate, everything just completely quiet, nothing going on. Harley said, 'Aah, let's just padlock the gate and put it on the report for the city manager,' and then I smelled it—" He paused, shook his head, muttered, "Shit," cleared his throat, and continued. "We started shining our lights around, following the fence line, and the smell kept getting stronger and then we saw . . . Christ, Jake, I'm afraid . . . he's not just dead, he's *mutilated*."

"You tried for a pulse?"

"Oh, sure. No pulse, no respiration. His pupils are dilated and his eyes are fixed, and . . . well, *look* at him."

Kneeling, I switched on my big Streamlight, squinting against the sudden glare. A young man's body sprawled, partially propped against a pile of plastic-covered cushions on the sandbag marking home plate. He looked young, boyish even, with full lips and round cheeks. A little *too* round, I thought—puffy—and the skin was taut and deeply flushed. I touched his face; it was cool and hard. His fingers were blue.

He wore a softball player's uniform, white with a thin gray stripe, tall red socks, a red cap with a bill. He smelled like blood, sweat, fried onions, and something else, musty or dusty, that I couldn't identify.

The upper body looked flung down, in a loose, jointless rag-doll way, arms trailing disordered across the dirt. The legs, in contrast, had been neatly arranged, carefully spread wide to show the gaping open fly of his uniform pants, where gore had clotted and turned dark. Blood oozing from the wound there had soaked the whole front of his suit, to the waist and above, and down almost to the knees; blood had seeped into the dirt under him, too, and a small colony of ants was already busy there. A softball bat had been inserted in the open front of his pants, the handle tucked inside the soaked fly, the larger end extending along the ground between his knees, in obscene outsize caricature of a penis.

"Jesus," I said softly. I pulled on surgical gloves. "Have you looked—?"

"Well as I could," Vince said, "without moving anything—"

I lifted the handle of the bat gingerly, tugged the open fly wider, shone the light carefully. Above me, Vince Greeley's breathing sounded ragged. I replaced the bat carefully.

"Are they gone?" Vince asked.

"Yup." I stood up, repressing an impulse to clutch my crotch, retrieved my briefcase, unzipped it, and got out my phone.

"You calling Pokey?" Vince asked. Adrian Pokornoskovic is the county coroner. He's not slow; he owes his nickname to the hapless inability of Rutherford law enforcement personnel to pronounce his last name. I can do it if I stop to think: "Po-kor-no-SKO-vich."

"BCA first. Hold my light, will you?" I punched one of my automatic-dial numbers and the pound sign and listened to the purr at the switchboard of the Bureau of Criminal Apprehension in St. Paul. A night recording offered me an interminable menu of choices. Squinting painfully in the flashlight beam, I punched a number, listened to some more choices, punched another number, and was finally rewarded by a live female voice saying, "Anderson."

"Jake Hines. Detective division, Rutherford. How are you?"

"Well, for somebody who's working a night shift on two

hours' sleep I'm not bad, thank you. What can I do for you?"

"I've got a truly nasty homicide here. We're going to need your help with this. Victim's unidentified so far, and the thing is he's been mutilated pretty badly—"

"Mutilated? Did you say mu—?"

"Uh, yes. His genitals are missing. Also the body's been posed—and there is a bat—"

"A what?"

"A softball bat. Carefully arranged in place of the missing penis. You understand what I'm saying? We're dealing with something really out of the ordinary here, Ms.—is it Dr. Anderson?"

"Grace will do fine, Jake." She sounded imperturbable. Was that her soothing technique from Psych Lab I? It wasn't working for me. Something about her seamless calm made me unreasonably irritated.

I counted five-four-three-two-one and said, "Grace. Okay. This is a request for your mobile crime lab, Grace. Quickly, please. Just as fast as you possibly can. It's imperative that your people see the crime scene just as we found it, and keeping it intact for very long is going to be close to impossible, because it's in a public park. I'm trying to express a sense of urgency here, Grace."

"I hear you, Jake. Both my vans are out right now, but I expect one of them back any minute. If they don't have too much off-loading to do, they can clean up and restock pretty fast. And I believe I can round up a fresh crew within, oh, about an hour, I think. If they beat the morning traffic, the trip should take, what, an hour and a half?"

"Just about. So two and a half, and it's, uh, two-thirty-five now, they should be here not much after five, right?"

"Give or take. Don't hold me to the minute, now. But I understand your concern, Jake, so be assured we'll give it our highest priority. Let's have that address now, okay?"

I gave her detailed instructions for finding the park, and the phone number downtown to call if they had any trouble finding it, and added, "And Grace? Pictures are going to be key here. Many, many pictures, pal. I wouldn't dare describe this to anybody without pictures to back me up."

"Sounds like you got yourself a winner, Jake. My other phone is ringing, 'bye."

I hung up and stared at the phone, thinking, Well, Jesus, Gracie, surely you can't be getting another phone call quite as titillating as this one, do you suppose? I yield to no one in my admiration of the Minnesota system; it allows a midsize town like Rutherford, with the limited technology that a tax base of a hundred thousand people can support, to tap into all the high-tech goodies that the state has up there in St. Paul. But sometimes the unshakable confidence of the big-city pros bothers me, like an itch I can't scratch. You call somebody in the predawn hours to report a client with a missing dick, you feel as if you ought to get at least a well-I-never.

To Vince I said, "You call for backup yet?"

"No. Not that I could get any tonight, probably, if my head was on fire. Three guys out with the flu, and Sunday night? Plus the Shrine circus is in town."

"Right. But still . . . you get off at, what, six-thirty? And you'll have paperwork to do on this, so you'd like to head in early—and that crime lab crew might not be ready to move the body till seven or even eight, and I gotta keep this park closed up tight till they're through . . . I better tell the desk I'm gonna need help here. Why is Harley staying over by the gate?" I asked while I dialed.

"Oh"—Vince's grin flashed briefly as he turned toward the streetlight—"he threw up when we found this guy, Jake. I guess it's his first homicide. Kind of spooked him, and now he's embarrassed, so I put him over by the gate to wait for you, and I suppose . . . he'd just as soon stay as far away as possible."

"Well, he's not going to learn anything over there. Better go get him, have him help you tape off, let's block every-thing from the gate over to the stands there. Don't let him walk near the body, Vince, okay? . . . Floyd?" The dispatcher came on with the harsh chatter of the console in the back-ground. "Listen, buddy, this is Jake, I'm here in Pioneer Park with Vince Greeley, and we're gonna need—" I lis-tened a minute to the dispatcher's tirade about short crews, three fights in bars, and a break-in. "Uh-huh. Wow. Terri-ble. Uh, lemme talk to the lieutenant, will you?"

Ed Gray took my request without comment, adding it to the steady flow of problems crackling in over his desk monitor. Hanging up, I felt a boost of escapist pleasure. Years ago, I did my stint on the night dispatch desk; I have grim memories of the alternating boredom and hysteria, the mounting anger and violence after midnight, and the predawn smells of puke and despair. I went back to rattling doors on graveyard, gladly, to get off the night dispatch desk. It wasn't the best deal I ever made; I'd have been turned loose a few months later, anyway, when the depart-ment reorganized and gave the dispatch desk to support personnel, with just one uniformed sergeant out front and a lieutenant running the show from the back office. Old-timers in the department think the new kids could use some of the insight you get from working night dispatch, though. We're like grandparents who walked three miles through snowbanks to school; we hated it, so it must have been good for us.

I stared blankly into the darkness for a minute, thinking. Then I punched another of my automatic numbers and heard the phone ring once, twice, and a half a third ring before the flat, shockproof voice of the chief said quietly, "McCafferty."

It's a tough call, deciding when to wake up the chief of police. There's nothing written in the training manual. And McCafferty's instructions on the subject aren't crystal clear, partly because the department has grown by a third since he took it over and sometimes he's too busy to fart. He knows he can't administer a hundred-plus cops and half again as many support personnel by staying hands-on with everybody. But he doesn't like to be left out of the loop on anything important, either. And while this homicide wasn't going to make a blip on the national screen, in Rutherford it was going to be huge. I thought it was better if he heard about it now.

"What's up?" McCafferty asked when I identified myself. Years of answering crisis calls have taught him to ask short questions and let the caller talk.

"I gotta damn strange homicide over here, Frank," I said. "In Pioneer Park. Be good if you took a look, I think, before everybody else gets here."

"Huh," he said. That's about as eloquent as he gets, usually. "Well . . . okay. Be there in a minute."

McCafferty was my training officer when I started on the Rutherford police force. My handgun intimidated me, in the beginning; it was weeks before I was an adequate shot. My uniform didn't fit right, and my lousy spelling made paperwork a nightmare. Also, because I was in the first wave of minority hires, many Rutherford people were shocked when they saw my face above a blue suit and a badge. Their reactions ranged from amusement to hostility. Frank helped me with all that, and much more.

It would be pleasant to report that I never forget how much I owe him, but in fact I have days, now, when I'd like to throw a six-pack at his head. I know he's under a lot of pressure because Rutherford's growing so fast, and the department has to grow with it, so I accept that he's impatient and pushy and can't seem to let people finish their sentences. But besides that, a lot of politics goes with the chief's job, and it doesn't sit pretty on a cop. Every time I hear him fire up up one of those sixty-nine-dollar phrases like "Rest assured, the department will be sensitive to blah blah blah," I want to stick a Glock in his ear and demand that he show me where he's hidden Frank McCafferty.

But faced with a nasty crime like this one, I figured it was best to get him into the picture early. He'd need some time to get his news releases ready. And before that, if I could jerk his investigator string just right, I was hoping he'd give me a little help. Frank has an eye like an outhouse rat for the small details that everybody else overlooks.

While I waited for him, I consulted my wallet card for the home phone number of the district attorney, Ed Pearce.

His call could have waited, but I had many calls to make and somebody had to be first, so I punished the politician. Or that was my intention, but the strong hello that rattled my ear came from Ed's wife, Doris. I love talking to Doris; she doesn't even try to disguise the fact that she's the power half of the pair. Besides managing the town's biggest travel agency, she directs many aspects of the DA's career. I explained that I was investigating a homicide in Pioneer Park, and had called because I believed the DA would want to stop by on his way to work to acquaint himself with the case. She told me she would relay my message. I didn't even think or arguing.

McCafferty eased his bulk through the gate as I hung up. He said a quiet word to Greeley and Mundt and then crunched heavy-footed along the gravel path toward me. The chief's large size is the subject of many jokes in the department: The municipal pool cover is a Frank blanket, thunder is a Frankie fart. I think he looks a little bigger than he is because his hands and feet are outsize for the rest of him. He's doing pretty well with his weight right now. A jock in his youth, he is doomed, in desk-bound middle age, to an ongoing battle with inappropriate metabolism and conducts intense daily negotiations with himself over beers, desserts, and a StairMaster. He moves with the confident ease of a man whose size has always settled most arguments without a fight, and he can still run if he has to, though it's true that the earth does shake.

"Whatcha got, Jake?" he asked.

"I've got a dead man here who's not a pretty sight," I said. "Looks as if he might have been killed in some kind of a ritual or . . . I don't know. Pretty weird."

"Oh?" He fixed his pale blue stare on me. Frank made chief the year before I moved up to the detective division; we have been over a few jumps together since he taught me where to hang my whistle, so he knows I didn't call him down here in the middle of the night just to jerk his chain. Still, when he gets you in the crosshairs like that, you want to be right. "Greeley and Mundt found it? What were they doing in the park at this hour?"

"They were doing a drive-by. Saw the gate standing open and came in to—"

"Male or female?"

"Huh? Oh, the victim. Male."

"Okay, how far've you gone with this?" he asked. "You called all the help you need?"

"Yep. BCA is sending a van, they should be here in a couple hours. Ed Gray's sending a couple of backup squads as soon as he can free them up. I've called the DA, and I'll call Pokey as soon as you and I are through. But before anybody else gets here, what I was wondering . . . You think you could take time to walk around this thing with me? I'd like to hear you describe it to me, and I'll take notes, okay? Because I have really never seen anything like this body before, and I wanna be sure I haven't missed anything." I had my spiral notebook on a clipboard, turned to an unmarked page.

"Well—sure. Okay. Where's the . . . ? Oh." McCafferty was silent a moment, and then said, "Holy Jesus." He stood quiet over the body for several minutes, moving his light occasionally, stooping once briefly. He straightened up, cleared his throat, and said, "Well, you're right, Jake, this is very unusual. Fortunately." Then, without preamble, he began.

"Victim is young, probably nineteen to twenty-three, I think, don't you? Caucasian. Light brown hair, pale skin with freckles, blue eyes, nice flat ears, medium build—" His flat midwestern inflection reduced the recitation to book-keeping. He described the awful wound, the gruesome parody of the softball bat, in a voice so matter-of-fact he might have been making a shopping list. Gratefully, I concentrated on my notes.

"Wearing a softball player's uniform, couple sizes too big." It was? I hadn't noticed that. Sure enough. "Don't they usually have their name on the pocket, and the position they play? This one's plain, no name. You look on the back yet?"

"No."

"Gimme a hand. Just easy, don't—There." Frank's flashlight played over the unadorned back of the uniform blouse. "Huh. No name on the back either. He looks a little too old to be a high school player, don't you think? Must be on a City League team. They play here last night?"

"Don't know. Have to check."

"You know this fella?"

"No. And Vince doesn't. You notice the marks on his neck?"

"Uh-huh. Looks like he mighta been choked before he was cut. Hope so, poor bugger. What's this?" Neatly pinned to the front of the uniform, just below the pocket, was a Polaroid picture of the crime scene, just as it appeared now. Frank straightened and fixed me again with his pop-eyed pale blue stare. "A picture? What the holy shit, Jake?"

"Now you see why I called you? You ever see anything like this, Frank?"

"No. Jesus Christ, no. I mean . . . okay, let's keep on, here. Body's leaning against a pile of cushions from some kind of outdoor furniture, light-colored plastic covers over foam rubber, looks like the cushions off a couple of benches or chaise longues. He's on top of the sack for home plate, on softball diamond number, uh"—his light swept the darkness till it picked out the number on the backstop—"number two. Don't see any marks on the ground here, from a dolly or cart or like that, or drag marks. Meaning he was killed right here? But no signs of struggle either, that I can see in this light. On the other hand, no trail of blood stains either. Swell, he dropped from the sky. Maybe you'll be able to see something when it gets light. *If* you can keep everybody from walking all over the place.

"Now, what else about the body? Third finger of left hand shows an indentation, like a missing wedding ring maybe." Bingo, I wondered if he'd catch that. I've got one like it. Mine is starting to fade, after six months. So probably the victim's been divorced or separated, for less than a year. Or maybe he's just cheating on his wife. So his wife caught him after a ball game and cut off his dong? Worth thinking about. "Cheap digital wristwatch, plastic band. What about a wallet?"

I shook my head. "This uni has no pockets in the pants. Usually each team has a locker or two—I'll get the super to show me in the morning."

"Okay. Jake, did you notice his shoes?"

"Shoes? Aren't they just standard black cross-trainers? With the—oh, I see what you mean. Leather. And metal cleats."

"Went out about ten, fifteen years ago, didn't they? These old clunkers?"

"Be damned. You're right. These look like the ones I wore in high school." It was my turn to stare blankly at Frank. "Anybody still play in these things?"

"Don't know. It's one more thing for you to find out. These cushions remind me of something, I have a feeling I've seen 'em before. Or some like 'em. Check for labels. Well, and prints of course, but you know how it is with plastic." Slippery, greasy, pebbled, hard to read. Not likely we'll get any decent prints off the cushions. But the bat, the picture, even the shoes might yield useable prints.

We stood silent a moment, then Frank stepped away from the body and said, "Okay. Let's say what we think we're looking at here, and then I gotta get going. I have to get press releases ready, and then I've got that awards breakfast for neighborhood crime watch people at seven-thirty . . . You start."

I turned to a fresh page and began listing. "Definite homicide, there's no way it could be anything else. Cause of death, I'd have to say uncertain. Obviously the wounds we see here could have killed him, but we don't know for sure that they did. Victim's identity unknown, but we'll probably have it as soon as I find some of the players from last night's game. Perp unknown. Motive unknown, but it must have been a doozy. Unusual aspects of the crime: sexual mutilation, body appears carefully posed, picture of crime scene attached to the body." I looked up. "What else?"

"No signs of a struggle, but no indication he was brought here either. Time of death might be a lot of help to you on this case, if you could get one. We know the body had to arrive on this playing field after the last game last night, but is that when he died? Hell of it is, you know, medical examiners don't like to call 'em very close. Too many variables.

"About that picture, Jake. I really hate that picture. Sexual mutilation's bad enough, but the picture makes it look like somebody having fun. It's so . . . playful. We might be dealing with a real kinkster here. Get St. Paul to search all their records for these two elements, the mutilation and the picture. See if they can match it up with anything they've seen up there lately. Doesn't seem likely this crime was done by anybody local, does it? If we had a weirdo like this around, we'd probably know it.

"Now, media," he went on. I stared into the dark and gritted my teeth. Frank was starting to tend the department's image. During our first week together in the squad car, he told me, "Police work is very straightforward, don't try to make a big deal out of it. Just keep your fly zipped and be sure you rattle the right doors." Sometimes lately I'd like to say it back to him.

"I'm going to call the editor of the paper, what's his name, Burgess," McCafferty said, "and Fred Task at the TV station, and ask them to look after this news release personally. We'll give them this: a dead John Doe, suspected homicide—well, no, homicide for sure—but perpetrator unknown, time of death unknown, cause of death unknown, but the police expect to have more details soon. That won't hold them for long, of course. But maybe you can get an ID, cause of death, something so you can spoon-feed 'em a few more details before the afternoon broadcasts. They get in kind of like a feeding frenzy, you know, if you don't keep giving them a little something new every day. I'm not gonna release any details yet on the mutilation, though, let's keep that to ourselves as long as we can, we don't want to fire up any copycats that might be out there, and besides it's going to alarm everybody, and what's the use? We can't issue any list of helpful suggestions for not getting your pecker cut off.

"And listen, there'll be no releases, ever, on that picture, till we get this perp. I want you to tell Vince and Harley, shut up about this. I know it's hard, folks at home expect to get the inside skinny, but we need to keep this in-house as long as we can. When their relief gets here, keep everybody outside the gate till you get the crime scene cleaned up. Ask Pokey to do the autopsy himself and walk the paperwork over, tell him don't fax it and don't put it in the database yet, okay?"

He glared at me like a stern parent on the first day of school, turned to go, then turned back to say, "You can have all the help you need on this, Jake. Full court press." He shook his head dolefully. "People are just gonna go . . . positively . . . apeshit." He stomped off toward the gate, looking aggrieved.

· TWO ·

ON THE FIRST RING, POKEY SAID, "OH, YAH?" LIKE SOME-
body disputing the price of onions. He's a light sleeper,
a small, taut Ukrainian immigrant who practices derma-
tology with two partners downtown. Usually, his coroner's
job in peaceful Rutherford yields a welcome stipend with
minimum disruption of his schedule. Mostly he certifies
cause of death for old people in rest homes and hospitals.

In ten years of Minnesota residence, the coroner's gut-
tural Russian accent has stayed pretty much intact. But his
vocabulary has acquired a rich overlay of American slang,
indiscriminately culled from his several generations of patients. Pokornoskovic loves the jazzy creativity of street English, but he never seems to realize that as some expressions
get hot, others go out of style. Everybody at the station has a

favorite Pokey quote; mine is, "Well, cripes, ain't that way cool?"

"Jake Hines, Pokey."

"Hey, Jake, what's shakin', baby?" He sounded jolly on principle, but he knew I wasn't calling in the middle of the night to talk about the weather. Pokey walked across large portions of Russia and Europe on his way to the United States, with interim stops in haystacks and sewage culverts. He is very hard to astonish. I told him what I had; he said, "Uh, Mmmm. Yah," took down the address, said, "See ya," and got off the phone.

It took a long time to wake Andy Dornoch, the director of parks and recreation. Finally his voice, sounding far-off and fragile, whispered, "Hello?" Feeling cruel, I explained to this barely awake bureaucrat why we needed to close the town's biggest park for several hours. I managed to describe the dead body, and the procedures that still had to be followed, without sharing any of the details McCafferty had prohibited. Andy listened silently till he understood, then cleared his throat and said he'd bring the keys over. He's not the kind to make a fuss. I told him I'd wait for him outside the front gate.

The sky lightened a little in the east while I stood there. Andy parked his five-year-old Taurus in front of me and got out in his deliberate, unhurried way, a big rawboned Scot, freckled all over, his bald dome fringed with pinkish gray curls. Greeley and I sometimes called him Zucchini Man; he was one of those passionate gardeners who bring you sacks full of vegetables in August, with little bouquets of zinnias and bachelor's buttons sticking out of the top.

At public gatherings in Rutherford, it always seemed to be Andy who was finding the extra tables and making the mike work.

He handed me a little padlock key first, saying, "Here, this is for all three fence gates, works the way they all do, you know?" Then he maneuvered a Yale key off a big metal ring, strung it on an old shoestring that he pulled out of his pocket, and gave it to me, saying, "This is for the front. Tie it onto your key ring now, so you won't lose it. It's a copy, so it's not an exact fit. It's pretty close, but you have to jiggle it back and forth a little, like this, till you feel it fit the tumblers, see?" He showed me, then said, "Now you do it," and watched while I showed him I could.

"How soon do you need this back?" I asked him.

"No hurry about the key, this is a spare. Just be sure you don't lose it, and get it back to me soon as you're done with it. Only control I got is keeping track of the keys. But listen, when can we get in the park? Head Start kids get here at eight."

"We'll do our best," I said, "but—if we're a little late can you put 'em someplace else for a while?"

"Kinda tough. They come by bus. From all around town."

"Well—we'll sure try, Andy, and I'll let you know just as soon as we're outta here."

"Ahh—well. Call my office, will you, as soon as you're out? I'll wait there till you call."

Pokey pulled his beat-up ragtop Jeep up to the curb while I was still fiddling with the gate. I let him in, and then wasted three minutes trying to relock the gate from inside. I tried to shove my fingers between the wire mesh and the frame, ripping several pieces of skin off the backs of my hands in the process and muttering gross profanities. Finally, I gave up, stepped outside, and locked it, and walked around to the little gate on Webster. By the time I got back to the body on the ground, Pokey was starting his preliminary examination. He shone his penlight into the victim's eyes, took his temperature, touched his cheeks and ankles gently, held his hands. He borrowed my Streamlight, to examine the wound between the victim's legs, then stared a long time at the marks on his neck.

The sky above the eastern trees turned blazing red. I heard the crunch of tires on gravel, looked through the gates, and saw the long white BCA step van pull into the semicircle in front. I ran around the outside corner of the block and opened up for them, pointed out the way to the softball fields, locked the gate again from outside, and trotted back around to the side gate. The driver had parked by the time I got back and was opening the wide rear doors.

"It's like a huge, beautiful tackle box," I told Pokey, "or the neatest tool shed I ever saw." The BCA van is a pleasure to look at, because it's well thought out. It's packed with shiny stainless steel cabinets full of gadgets: vials and pipettes and tweezers and lenses, spotless gloves and gowns, quick-fold boxes and glass jars. Along one bulkhead, paper evidence bags are clipped onto a plastic line by sizes, with their red strings hanging down like some nerdy hula skirt. A sailor would go crazy over the lashings and battens, the clips and snaps and bungee cords, that keep the outfit tidy.

"Jake Hines," I said, sticking out my hand to the driver.

"Trudy Hanson," she said, flashing a grin that boasted many dimples. She looked like an ad for some kind of vitamin supplement, with beautiful strong white teeth, round cheeks the color of ripening peaches, and wheat-colored hair in a braid down her back. She began pulling cameras and film out of a cupboard, which gave me an opportunity to admire the way she filled out her jeans.

"Jimmy Chang," said her front-seat passenger, shrugging into a lab coat. "I think we've met once before, Jake." Slender, handsome and intense, Chang's Chinese-Hawaiian biochemist pulling shifts at the State Crime Lab while he works on his Ph.D. in forensic pathology at the university. He did the blood and tissue analysis that sorted out an accidental poisoning death we had last year. "I'll start with blood samples, I guess. Where's the—oh."

It was remarkable how closely his first reaction to the body matched McCafferty's. They had both been to plenty of death scenes, but this one shocked them. The sexual mutilation and the mockery of the picture, contrasted with the wholesome ordinariness of the softball uniform, struck everybody as gratuitously brutal. Jimmy Chang covered his discomfiture by busy work with gloves and gear. Trudy set up two floodlights and silently began firing off a flash every few seconds.

Pokey began negotiating with Chang for the earliest possible removal of the body to the lab. "You can get hair and blood samples better down there, you dig? And sooner we start autopsy, by crackey, closer we call time of death."

Jimmy's handsome face took on the bemused expression people always get during a first exposure to Pokey rhetoric. I left them negotiating and started another outside sprint for the front gate, where I saw the assistant DA standing. I was starting to sweat. Maybe I'll create a fad, I thought, aerobic investigator.

"Yo, Milo," I said, "Big Ed too busy with politics to mess with a murder?"

"You said that. I did not," Milo Nilssen said.

"Come around to the side gate, will you?" I asked him, "Messing with this big front gate is wearing me down." He followed me around the corner, gabbing companionably.

"Ed's on his way to breakfast with your boss, actually," he said. "They're giving attaboys to those neighborhood crime watch winners. How do they stand all that bullshit? Every time I start getting ambitious for higher office, I think about all that rubber chicken and pancakes, and I just— Ooh, you called the BCA crew, huh?"

"Yup." I went over the timeline of the crime so far and gave him a quick rundown of the list of unknowns, adding, "And listen, Milo, all the information on this case has to stay between you and me, Frank and Ed, till further notice. Nothing in the database, and keep your notes locked up. We're hoping for an early suspect, and we need a few details held back."

"You got a suspect, Jake?" He shot me one of his keen-eyed raptor looks. Sometime last year, Milo discovered that his hawkish glance, out of pale amber eyes rimmed with white lashes, has the power to startle, sometimes eliciting information nobody intends him to have. It seemed like a neat ploy when I saw him do it in court, but now I resented being on the receiving end of the trick.

"No, Milo. You got a better idea?" I asked shortly.

"No. Hey. No offense." Milo has a sequenced reaction to any challenge: he shoots his cuffs, smooths his hair back, grooms his mustache, licks his lips, and looks at his watch. By the time he finished his atonement ritual we'd arrived at playing field two, and Milo got his first look at the body. Abruptly seizing my upper arm in a surprisingly powerful grip, he whispered, "Omigod, Jake, omigod omigod—" His freckles stood out vividly in his suddenly ashen face. To my astonishment, I found myself patting Milo Nilssen's hand.

Pokey and Jimmy had pulled a gurney out of the van and were fiddling with the braces on the folding legs. Jimmy got a body bag out of a compartment, shook it open, and asked Trudy, "What say? Got enough pictures?"

"I think so." She looked at me. "Unless there's anything in particular—?"

"The snapshot," I said. "Take a closeup of the Polaroid snapshot, will you? And did you get plenty of shots of the area around the body? About six feet all around? Sometimes things show up in photos that I never saw at all at the site." I had looked in vain for tracks and blood spatters while I waited for the van, and had gone over the ground again in the last ten minutes, in full light, with no success.

We all stood back while Trudy squeezed off a few more shots. Efficient and relaxed, she seemed to have all the details of her job so completely in hand that she could easily afford to accommodate the people around her. It was a pleasure watching her work. Come to think of it, it was a pleasure just watching her. I noticed that Pokey and Milo thought so, too. In her breezy, unmade-up way, the BCA photographer was a dish.

Jimmy picked up the bloody softball bat gingerly with the ends of his gloved fingers, dropped it in an evidence bag, handed it to me, and said, "You've got a vapor box here at the station, haven't you? Good, then you might as well check for prints on this. The cushions, too. Well, and the picture, I guess—" He unpinned it from the uniform and dropped it in another bag. Then I lent a hand in the grim and intricate business of bagging the corpse and boosting it onto the cart.

Pokey led off in his car, the van following, while I locked the padlock on the side gate. Milo stuffed his hastily scribbled notes in his briefcase and walked out through the front with me.

"I might as well go straight to work," he said, forlornly, "I sure as hell don't want any breakfast after this."

I locked the big creaky front gate one last time, followed the other three vehicles west on Eighth Street for a couple of blocks, then peeled off and drove to the station. I checked the bat, picture, and cushions into the evidence room, with a request for fingerprint workups ASAP. I grabbed two frosted doughnuts and a cup of coffee from the break room and took them along. Getting back in my car, I remembered I hadn't called Andy Dornoch yet. Greedily sipping coffee, I punched up his phone number, put the car in gear, and started toward the lab. Andy grabbed his phone off the hook before it finished its first ring and growled, "Dornoch."

"Yo, Andy," I said, "Pioneer Park is all yours."

Andy was relieved. "Head Start teacher's can give grief you wouldn't believe," he said. "All those little screamers make 'em testy."

I told him I needed some information, and he made a list: the name of the caretaker who should have locked up after last night's game; the names of the teams that played last night, and their captains' names; the numbers of the lockers they would have used.

"I believe I have the name of this year's City League manager, would that help?" He rummaged through his files while I waited, came back, and said, "Lou Bjornson. Works at Heilemann's Dairy. I've got home and work numbers; you ready?"

"Wait a minute, I'm at a four-way stop," I said, and he grumbled, "God, I hate car phones. And answering machines—"

"Okay, I'm all set, shoot."

"Faxes, modems, VCRs, I hate 'em all," he said. "All they're doing is making life so damn complicated I can't get any work done—"

"What's your stand on the internal combustion engine, Andy?" I asked him. I wrote down the numbers he gave me, while a spectacularly pretty girl, wearing four earrings in each ear, gunned her Lexus across two lanes of traffic to beat me out at the next traffic signal. It probably would have wrecked her day to know how little I cared. Since I use my car as much for an office as for transportation, I have come to think of red lights as stenographic pit stops. I sat contentedly at the Broadway crossing, dialing the first number Andy Dornoch had given me.

Lou Bjornson, his wife said snappishly, was in the shower. Pressed, she grudgingly guessed she could call him. I maneuvered through hell-bent morning traffic from Broadway to Second Avenue, barely survived a left turn onto Fourth, and pulled into the parking lot behind the lab, while a Bjornson family screaming match assaulted my left ear. Lou and Mrs. Lou debated the relative merits of his coming to the phone or putting it where the sun would never shine on it, while a couple of little Bjornsons tried to destroy each other somewhere nearby. Finally a grumpy male voice said, "Yeah?"

"Lou Bjornson?"

"Yeah, whaddaya need?"

"Jake Hines, Lou, I'm a detective with the Rutherford police department. I'm looking for a little information. Are you the manager of the city softball league?"

"Yeah, I am. But if you're selling—"

"Not selling anything, Lou." I tried a firmer tone. "I just need answers to a couple of questions, please. Did any City League teams play in Pioneer Park last night?"

"Yeah, sure, uh—lessee. The early game was Lloyd's Van Lines against the Hi-Life Bar, boy, what a fiasco that was—"

"A little mismatched, huh?"

"Tell me about it. I think the final score was twenty-eight to two. And then at eight o'clock Dan's Electric played the Roxy, damn good game. Why, whaddaya lookin' for?"

"Well . . . Lou . . . here's the thing—" I told him about a body in the park, and the uniform, selecting my details carefully. Lou had a typical layman's reaction to news of death; most of his brain cells quit functioning. His voice rose about half an octave, and his surly assurance evaporated. He nattered inanely about start-up dates and new players, and dead-centered on trying to remember anyone showing up in an unmarked uniform.

"We've got rules against it, y'know, but sometimes at the start of the season—"

"Lou," I interrupted, "Could you get me the names of the captains on those four teams? And their phone numbers? How about bringing them to the Hampstead County Pathology Lab on your way to work? It's at 302 East Fourth.

I'll meet you at the front door. I'm Jake Hines, five-eleven, black hair, brown eyes, I'll show you my badge. Well, if you're late for work, have your boss call me, and I'll verify that you were doing a big favor for the police, okay? Really, it'll help a lot. Thanks."

I finished my doughnuts and coffee while I made a few more notes. Then I stowed my notebook and phone in my briefcase and got out to stand by the front door of the lab, waiting for Lou Bjornson. I felt vaguely displaced in the cheerful ordinariness of the morning. People were picking their teeth, finishing their makeup, and sneaking through stoplights on the last of the amber. Last night in Pioneer Park began to seem like an evil dream. Across the street, on the wide lawn at Methodist Hospital, tulips splashed a patch of jolly color alongside the front steps and fat squirrels chased each other up and down oak trees.

Damp mulchy air caressed me, making me suddenly, inappropriately horny. I began to identify with one particularly ardent gray squirrel. "Go for it, big fella," I silently urged him. "You can catch her if you try." He poured on speed, but she beat him to the chokecherry bush and disappeared.

Lou Bjornson drove like a cowboy, rounding the turn into the driveway with a squealing flourish. Rubber steamed on the blacktop under his sliding stop. He looked at me and then past me, as people often do, expecting a more mainstream face for law enforcement, but I had my badge ready and held it up. He handed out a penciled list on lined paper, and was already shifting into reverse when I leaned in to say, "Lou, what time do you get off work today?"

It took skill and patience to elicit Lou's promise to stop back at the lab after work. He did not want to look at any dead man, least of all a dead man he might know. I layered on shame and praise in equal measure. Finally, reluctantly, Lou promised to come back at five-thirty.

By the time I got inside and found Pokey and Jimmy, they had transferred the body to a high stainless steel table and were carefully peeling off the bag. They weighed and measured the body, noted skin, hair, and eye color, a tattoo on the upper arm, an old scar on the thigh. Pokey took the wristwatch and a pinkie ring, the only personal effects he found, bagged and tagged and listed them. Trudy went out to the van and came back with her fingerprint kit; she fitted a strip of high-gloss print paper onto the spoonlike plate and laid out ink, pad, and cleaning materials. She put a fresh roll of film in her camera and checked the battery on the flash.

I helped Jimmy remove the uniform, cutting it carefully along the seams. I wanted to keep it, to show to Lou Bjronson and his players. Jimmy said he had to take it to St. Paul to do hair and fiber analysis on it first. It was the first of several competing needs we would negotiate, standing over the pitiful corpse in the harsh, uncompromising glare of fluorescent overhead lights. Jimmy got the suit first, of course. BCA, once we've called them in on a case, has the clout to win all the arguments. Before he bagged and tagged it, Trudy took a couple of extra pictures of it for me.

"I'll get it back to you by the end of the week," Jimmy promised.

"But we can check the shoes for prints here, right?" I asked, wanting desperately to keep the strange leather shoes, but Jimmy said, "No, I'd better do soil samples and stain analysis."

The dead man wasn't wearing any underwear. No shorts, no jockstrap, nothing.

"That's kind of unusual," Jimmy said.

"Unheard of," I said. I was keeping my notes strictly factual, trying to avoid the trap of early conjecture. But I put an exclamation point by my no-underwear notation.

"Another thing you can write down there, Jake," Pokey said, bending to examine the wound between the legs, "is, this cutting wasn't done with no scalpel." He and Jimmy began a spirited debate over the probable weapon, settling eventually for a French knife or fish-filleting tool in a not very skillful hand. They went on to an examination of the marks on the neck, which seemed to interest Pokey particularly. He helped Trudy take pictures of the marks from all angles, then invited me to take a closer look.

"See this mark? It's thin and dark, and goes straight around. Was made by wire, not rope." He turned to Trudy. "You want to get fingerprints now? While Jimmy gets hair and blood and tissue samples, yah? And then we boogie along here and see if we can decide what makes him die."

Sidelined by lack of expertise, I went back to making phone calls. The first three people on Lou's list were already gone to work; I got two no-answers and one housewife who took a message. My fourth call woke a bartender who had played for the Hi-Life team in the early game last night and then worked his shift at the bar; he was so nearly comatose he dropped the phone twice while he tried to pick it up. I got his promise to call the station later and let him go back to sleep.

I'll have to call all these guys back tonight, I thought despondently. That's the thing about detective work, that feeling of never being finished. It's like selling insurance; there are always a few more calls you really ought to make. Sometimes I remember my years in the blue uniform longingly. Work your eight hours and go home, and whatever's left over is somebody else's problem. The long, irregular hours of the detective division were one cause of the friction in my marriage, no question about it. Nancy hated the unexpected phone calls, the coming home late for dinner, the running down Saturday morning to clear up a few things.

Of course what she really hated were the nights I didn't come home at all. But what was near the end. When we were always fighting, unless we weren't speaking.

We signed a mutual-consent divorce decree a little more than six months ago, but I can't seem to leave it behind. I keep going back over it in my mind. We started out so sweet. How could we make such a pile of garbage in only four years? My brain still slides into recycle mode sometimes, playing a continuous feedback loop of the mistakes and cruelties and demeaning fights that rocked that final year. It feels like my delivery system's crashing in some vast power outage at the main grid, maybe taking the whole Midwest and parts of the lower Mississippi Valley down with it.

I've learned an escape trick, though; I hold my breath and focus on an imaginary blank white space in the middle distance. It isn't anything; that's the point. Nothing. After a few seconds, my computer boots up again. I let out my breath, clipped the team lists inside the front cover of my spiral notebook, and answered my ringing phone.

"Andy Dornoch, Jake. Mel Grieve was the late caretaker last night, and he claims he *did* lock up after the last game."

"Yeah, so, you believe him?"

"Well, he's a good man, been with us eight years. So, one of two things, I guess. He thought he had the shackle pushed in far enough to catch and he didn't, or—well, you know, Jake, padlocks are pretty standard, they're not that hard to open with a master. We put 'em on so the kids won't come in and goof around and drown themselves, but a determined guy who knew what he was doing could get through 'em all right."

"Sure. You find my team names?"

"You bet. Mel's got 'em for you. Mel took care of the lockers and showers last night, too. He's on again this afternoon, he'll show them to you whenever you can meet him there."

"At two o'clock," I said. "Thanks, Andy."

Trudy finished her fingerprint pictures then and brought me a set. I faxed them to the station. The techie wasn't busy, so I got an answer in a few minutes: no match in Rutherford.

"So, Trudy, let's get yours on the way to St. Paul," I said.

"Be better if I carry them back and put them in the system myself," Trudy said. "One for BCA and one for the FBI. Sometimes, if they're busy up there, the incoming stuff off the faxes gets put off till last."

I checked my watch: ten o'clock. Shouldn't somebody be missing this guy by now? I called the station to check for missing person reports.

"Nope, nothing," Mabel Houser said, "pretty quiet this morning, actually. Hennessey rescued a three-year-old boy off a roof, got his butt full of slivers." She giggled. "Hennessey, I mean. The kid was fine. Sheets and Franklin brought in ol' Hogbreath Haley, wouldn't it be nice if he could turn up missing for a while? He was peeing on the front steps of Saint Francis when Father Brennan opened the door for seven o'clock mass. Father asked him to leave, and he got aggressive, so we've got him in the tank." Her voice dropped when she asked, "So, Jake, you working on that homicide, huh? From the park last night? How's it going?"

"Okay. We're doing the autopsy now." The downside of a low crime rate is that the few homicides we do have get everybody's attention fast.

"Mabel, did anything come back from the pawnshops on that stuff from the Porter break-in?" I wanted to deflect her questions, and besides, I devoutly wished I might have something to report when Mrs. Porter called me this afternoon, as she surely would. Since her house had been forcibly entered through a side window last week, Millicent Porter had called me every day. Tearfully and repeatedly, she had described how irreplaceable the stolen items were. Last Friday she had reminded me that her sterling silver serving spoons were over a hundred years old.

"My grandmother brought them out from Pennsylvania with her when she came here as a bride," she quavered, her outrage building as it did every afternoon, "and when I think about them in the hands of those *criminals*—" I assured her I had extended the search to all the pawnshops in the Twin Cities. It was just something to say; I had done that the first day after the break-in.

Mabel said none of the pawnshops had called. Then Jimmy beckoned, and I put my phone away.

"We're ready to go," Jimmy said. "Most of my test results

will be available tomorrow, Jake, but we don't overnight the stuff, so you may not get it till Thursday or even Friday. If you need answers sooner, call the bureau. If there's anything you don't understand when you do get the test results, call me at one of these numbers." He handed me a card with four numbers on it. Jimmy Chang lives a complex life, divided between the crime lab and his student and teaching functions at the university.

"I'll FedEx your pictures later today," Trudy said. "You'll have them tomorrow. Fingerprint work should be finished by late this afternoon. They might not call right away, if they're busy, so if nobody identifies the victim by this afternoon you can call this number"—she gave me a card—"by four o'clock or so, and they'll tell you if they found anything. Okay?" She treated me to another of her agreeable, dimpled smiles and asked, "Anything else we can do for you before we go?"

"Sure you can't stay for lunch?" She looked at her watch and her partner; Jimmy shook his head and began packing gear out to the van.

"Drive careful out there, sweetheart," Pokey told her, "don't let them crazies run over you, yah?" Trudy giggled as she zipped up the last of her many Dacron bags.

To me, Pokey said, "I'll have some tentative skinny for you pretty quick."

My body had begun sending urgent messages, reminding me that it had been working ten hours on two doughnuts. I asked him, "How about doing some of your paperwork while we eat lunch? Okay if I go on and get us a booth at Victor's?" Victor's is a quiet family restaurant on Second Avenue, with old wooden booths and good meat loaf. I had snarfed down the entire contents of a bread basket and was starting on my salad by the time the doctor slid into the seat across from me.

"Time of death first," Pokey said, as soon as he'd ordered. "Well, of course you know officially it's gotta be whenever your guy found him there in the park, when was that?" He filled in a blank and sat back. "How long he'd been there on the ground is easy, too: more than ten minutes and less than twelve hours. He had flies' eggs in his eyes and nose. Takes those little buggers about ten minutes, usually, to find a body and get their eggs laid. No maggots hatched out yet, that takes about twelve hours."

"Gosh, you're fun to have lunch with," I muttered. The doctor grinned delightedly. "Yah, sure beats tellin' lies about sex and money, huh? Actual time of death, is good question. Sometime between ten o'clock last night and when your guy found him, give or take who knows how much. His temperature was ninety when I got there at five, they usually lose one to two degrees an hour. Rigor mortis was just starting, that's four to six hours. Usually. Weather can change it, but this time of year? Pretty close to book.

"Now, cause of death, I'm not gonna fill that in till we get BCA report. Might as well wait till all those fancy tests tell us did he have any drugs inside him, alcohol. Poison, whatever."

"Okay," I said, spooning sour cream onto a baked potato with a generous hand, "but whaddaya *think*, Pokey?"

Adrian Pokornoskovic executed a three-stage Eastern European shrug and turned his hands palm upward. "Most ways, looks like somebody strangled him first, then did funny business with family jewels. Face is congested and red, from blood vessels filling up. Seems like it should be redder, but . . . he was propped up there maybe several hours, drained a lot of blood out through that hole between his legs. Had some of those little dark red specks inside eyelids, from hemorrhages, that's typical of choking. Marks on neck go straight around. Neck shows deep contusions, throat has damage to thyroid cartilage. Coulda been strangled with wire cable, light cord, something small but strong like that."

Pokey twined spaghetti on his fork thoughtfully. "One thing interesting, Jake . . . soles of his feet were purple. And turned white when I poked 'em, then pretty soon got purple again. Seems about right for timing. Lividity not quite fixed yet. Usually means six to eight hours dead. But soles of feet?" The doctor leaned back in the booth, regarding me brightly.

"Is real humdinger, yah?" he mused. "Guy who just got strangled gets up and stands around for a couple hours?"

· THREE ·

GEORGE HAPWORTH WAS STIFLING A YAWN WHEN I POKED my head through the window of the evidence room at one o'clock. Record keeping is good duty when you're critically hungover or have a ton of paperwork to catch up on. Other days, watching that clock tick while you stand guard over bins full of lost purses and stolen bikes is enough to drive anybody bananas. Hapworth had a thriller clipped to the second shelf of his podium. He hustled up to the window, plainly hoping for distraction.

"Happy, have they done the print work on my stuff yet?" I asked.

"Just getting ready to run it now," Hapworth said. "Kranz checked it out five minutes ago."

I hurried around the corner of the little cupboard-lined storeroom where Kranz and Green were getting ready to run the test. Our fingerprint box is our own design; we found a plastics fabricator here in Rutherford to make it out of Plexiglas. It's a cube about three by three by eight, with electrical cord emerging from one corner and an exhaust pipe on top connected to the building sewer vent.

Ollie Green had just finished cleaning the panes of the box inside and out; now he plugged in the little hot plate that's fixed in one corner. He squeezed a couple of drops of Super Glue into a bottle cap and put the cap on the hot plate, along with a small tin cup full of water.

Nick Kranz, wearing surgical gloves, was pulling the staples out of tagged evidence bags. He laid each bag on the long tile-topped counter by the sink, put its own tags on top of it, then put a note on top of the tags reminding himself what went in each bag.

"You don't believe what I wrote on the tag?" I asked.

"Some of these bozos, I can't always read their writing," Kranz said. He tactfully kept his criticism general, but we both know that my handwriting looks like a sad accident in a hen-house. He carried the softball bat and the little Polaroid picture to the Plexiglas box and asked his partner, "Whaddaya say, 's it ready?"

"Smells like it. Let's get it closed up before we start to gag."

It's one of those simple but revolutionary discoveries: Super Glue, heated, emits a vapor that combines with human skin oil to turn fingerprints dark gray. The water in the cup adds just enough humidity to enhance the process. The prints come up clear and plain, and they don't disintegrate if they're jarred, or blow away in a breeze, the way dusted prints sometimes do.

On big stationary items—doors, walls, floors—we still have to dust, hope the dust sticks, and go through the laborious process of transferring the dust to lifting tape and coating that with clear plastic. But anything portable, up to the size of a rifle, can go in the box. After it's been in there for a few minutes with the Super Glue bubbling on the little coffee heater, any latent fingerprints will be permanently etched in gray. Then you can match them to pictures, if that's convenient, or take pictures at your leisure and match the photos.

"You used to use iodine, sometimes, for small stuff, didn't you?" I asked Kranz.

"Iodine crystals, yeah," Kranz said. "But the prints fade so fast, you've gotta be right there with the camera or you lose 'em. And I hated all that puffing and blowing through the gun, and you had to be so careful about storing the crystals airtight, or the good stuff evaporated. It's easier just to throw a tube of glue in the drawer, run out and buy another one when you need it.

"Also, you know how when you dust a print and lift it, usually it won't hold any more dust? If you need a second set of prints, forget it, there's just not enough skin oil left to hold anything. But once a print's been fumed up good with Super Glue, y'know, Jake, those little etchings turn into regular dust magnets, and you can make as many sets as you want."

The downside is the toxicity of cyanoacrylate vapor, the glue ingredient that clings to latent prints. Ingenuity and a great deal of duct tape went into venting our box with flexible plastic hose, and connecting that to the vent pipe for the building's sewer.

Also, the stability of the fingerprints, so prized at the station, seems somewhat less attractive to the rightful owners when evidence is at last returned to them. In fact an ongoing departmental revenge fantasy revolves around Super Glue technology and anybody's current nemesis. Kranz, for instance, longs for an excuse to boil up a double dose of Super Glue in the vanilla leather interior of a Mercedes belonging to F. Whitfield Collier, an arrogant defense attorney who once humiliated him in court. The squad room has been entertained more than once by a tableau of Kranz handing back the keys, smiling innocently, saying, "Oh, golly, I guess those prints will be kind of hard to get off. Sorry about that."

The Polaroid picture remained pristine. The softball bat turned gray all over, from the mingled fingerprints of ten seasons' ball players. The cushions came out mostly clean, with some unidentifiable smudgy blurs in a couple of the corners.

"Where would we be without science?" I asked them, and went back out to my car.

Mel Grieve was standing in front of the locker rooms, checking his watch, when I stopped in front of him at 2:05. He looked like one of those incredibly fit seniors who are always playing tennis in TV ads for gated housing developments. He had snowy hair above bright blue eyes, a strong, straight body, and a ruddy complexion. A large ring of keys hung from the right side of his belt, and a leather pouch of tools clinked against his left hip.

He looks familiar, I thought. Then I realized: he reminded me of the school janitor I had idolized when I was in third grade. He used to let me ride on his cleaning cart sometimes, and once I got to squirt cleaning fluid on the windows while he wiped.

"Mr. Dornoch said you'd want to see the lockers," Grieve said. "Right in here. Nothing in 'em, though."

"This is just how you found them?" I asked, aimlessly opening and closing the six empty metal cupboards.

"Yup. Kinda unusual, really. Four teams played last night. That many guys, usually somebody forgets something. But not a thing today. Nothing in the showers either."

"And you locked up after last night's games? What time was that?"

"Eleven-oh-five when I started. I do the side and back gates first, and I usually start with the one you found open, on Webster. Then I do the one at the back there, on Eighth Street, and then the side gate on Eleventh Avenue. That way I walk all the way around the park and check for stragglers before I lock up the big front gate on Ninth Street. It was just after eleven-fifteen when I finished locking up the front last night."

"You know," I said, "I locked that padlock on Webster this morning, but I was in such a hurry then—could we look at it together now?"

We walked together toward the gate, passing repeatedly from sun through dappled shade. With last night's horror cleared away, Pioneer Park was restored to its usual pretty peacefulness, the tall trees throwing patches of shade over the playing fields and swing sets. As we went by playing field two, I saw that fresh sand had been raked over the bloody spot by home plate. In the sunshine beyond the jungle gym, a double line of Head Start children formed a semicircle around their teacher and began some shrill chant in unison.

"Head Start kids still here?" I asked him. "Thought Andy said they came first thing Monday morning."

"We got three groups on Monday, one right after the other," Grieve said. "Keeps us all hoppin'. They have to stay right on schedule or the kids'll mix in together, and the teachers have a heck of a time sortin' 'em out."

At the Webster Avenue entrance, the locked padlock dangled from the two looped ends of a wire cable at the top of the woven steel gate.

"It seemed to me it was working all right," I said. "You haven't noticed it jamming up or anything—?"

"Nah. We oil these babies regular. You have to, when a lock's outside like this. See, I'll show you—" He unlocked the padlock, slid the pivoting shackle in and out a couple of times, locked it again, and offered me the passkey. "Wanna try it?" I unlocked and locked it again; the key turned easily, and the shackle slid smoothly into place. I looked at the cable and asked him, "You got a spare one of these?"

"Oh sure. Have to keep spares, they disappear every so often. You want one?"

"Could I have this one? And you replace it? I'll bring it back."

"Don't see why not. Mr. Dornoch said help you any way I could." Grieve unlocked the cable, handed it to me, and added, "Oh—he said to give you this list of players."

"Ah, yes, thanks." I stuffed both items into my bulging briefcase.

"You're welcome." Grieve suddenly leaned close and whispered, "You found a dead guy here in the park last night, huh?"

"Yes, we did, Mr. Grieve," I said. "Could I ask you, did you see anything unusual last night? Anybody that seemed to be kind of lurking around?"

He considered. "Had to run a couple of boys out of the men's toilet, they were making a mess out of the paper towels and writing on the mirrors with soap. But I guess you're looking for something a lot more serious than pranks, aren't you?"

"Afraid so. We'd be concerned about anybody that seemed to be waiting around for the players, especially somebody you're not used to seeing around the games."

He considered. "No—uh-uh. Can't think of anybody like that last night."

"Well, guess I better get going." I turned toward my car.

"Boy, I don't like this *at all*," Grieve said, crunching after me along the gravel. "Somebody getting killed, right here where I work? Half my shift is at night, after dark. I mean, how would you like it?" He shook his head gravely. "And you don't have any kind of a line on the fella that did it yet?"

"Not yet," I said.

"Better get down to business then," Mel Grieve said, "and forget all that foolishness with the bear."

"Bear?"

"Yeah, that silly bear that always marches in parades with a shovel, waste of the taxpayers' money for a grown man to be dressing up like that and throwing out candy—"

"That's the Forest Service, Mr. Grieve. Not the police."

"It's all the government, ain't it? Better cut out the foolishness and get this fella locked up so the rest of us can have some peace, hear?"

"We'll sure do our best, Mr. Grieve," I said, "and hey, listen, thanks for everything."

Mabel paged me as I turned north on Webster; when I answered, she gave me the number of Heilemann's Dairy and told me to ask for Lou Bjornson.

He came to the phone from some clanking distance filled with echoes.

"I found two guys from teams that played last night," he said. "One of 'em works here, and the other one's across the street at Peese's Lighting, and what we thought is, if you could meet us at that lab on our break time, we could all take a look."

"Terrific, Lou," I said. "When?"

"Fifteen, twenty minutes be okay?"

"Perfect," I said, and changed to the left-hand lane to go back to the lab instead of straight ahead to the station. I sat in the lab parking lot waiting for them, dialing numbers off Mel Grieve's list. Nobody was home, but I left two messages.

The three men came together, in Lou's car. He made his Indy 500 approach again, squealing his tires on the turn and then braking so hard for the stop that his passengers' heads snapped forward. The man must have to replace his tires once a year.

It was hard getting the three of them through the front door of the lab; nobody wanted to go first. They got silent and started looking shocked as they approached the covered mound on the tall steel table, before they ever saw anything. Their features were tight with apprehension as the sheet was pulled away. But they all brightened up, in obvious relief, as soon as the dead man's face was uncovered.

"Never saw him before," Lou said, and the two others echoed him gratefully. This man had not been on their teams, they stated positively. He was nobody they knew. Don Pfluge had played in the early game, Jason Dooley in the later one. This man had not been in either.

"And by now, I've met pretty much everybody that's going to play in the league this year, and I don't know this guy," Lou said. He was getting his cool back. His dread of finding a dead friend on the table was behind him now, and I could see that he was beginning to realize he had a helluva barstool yarn to go with the beers after work.

I mentioned the unmarked uniform again. Neither Don nor Jason could remember seeing anybody play without his ID sewed into his shirt. When I described the old leather shoes with metal cleats, they shook their heads incredulously.

"Maybe in pickup games out in the smaller towns," Dooley said. "But the City League? Plenty of guys practice hard all spring and *still* don't make these teams. We've got some pretty heads-up players, Jake. Sharp guys. You see any of our play-offs last fall?"

"I saw the semifinal between O'Toole's Bar and Dan's Electric," I said. "I still think that double play in the fourth inning shoulda been one on and one out—" We left the building contentedly rehashing an umpire's call from eight months ago. In Rutherford, old guys who can't remember where they put the car keys can recall, precisely, close plays from their youth.

On the way back to my office I left the padlock cable, in an unsealed evidence bag, with Pokey's receptionist. My note said, "Could one of these have been the murder weapon?"

"Just please give it to him before his next patient, will you?" I asked her. "And then phone me his answer, yes or no."

Back at the station, I took my ritual afternoon call from Millicent Porter.

"This is the third time today I've called you," she said peevishly. "Why aren't you ever in your office?" She was beginning to think I was never going to find those hoodlums who had ransacked her house, she said; "My beautiful house that I've worked my whole life for, and now it doesn't even feel like it belongs to me any more." She bet those thieves were sitting around laughing at her, *right here in Rutherford.*

"And I mean, if a person isn't safe in *Rutherford* any more," Mrs. Porter asked me, "well, what's the *use*?"

I assured her that the partial thumbprint we had taken from her front doorjamb was being forwarded to the FBI. The law was casting a widening net for her rugs and spoons. Yes, and the picture frames and the punch bowl, with her mother's initials, yes, I would not forget.

By the time I hung up, I had a message from Pokey. It said, "Could be." I clipped it inside my notebook, saw it was four o'clock, and called BCA. I asked for fingerprints division, waited a long time, and was just deciding to hang up when a voice said, "Angela."

I said, "Jake Hines, Rutherford," and she said quickly, "Oh, yeah, hold on a sec," and gave me, at last, a break. They had a match on my prints.

"Your victim's name is James Wahler," Angela told me. "We had him on file here because he did a stretch in the Red

Wing Juvenile Detention Center, let's see, seven years ago. Pleaded to felony shoplifting in Minneapolis, did six months, got a conditional release to his mother in Rutherford. They used to still do that then, now they don't even pretend the mothers can control 'em. Anyway he was charged with car theft in Austin a couple of years later, but the charges were dropped. Nothing since. He was fingerprinted both times, and this set matches both of those. Three complete sets, all taken by professionals, so your ID is pretty close to a hundred percent. Want copies?"

"Please. And thanks for the quick job."

Looking for support team help, I peered around the office and found Mabel Houser typing traffic citations into department records. It wasn't hard to persuade her to take a break from that and come help me run James Wahler's name and prints through MINCIS, the Minnesota Crime Information System. We found no record of adult arrests in Minnesota.

"I'd like to start looking for relatives here in town," I told her. "Will you go ahead and try NCIC?" Sometimes there's a wait at the National Crime Information Center, and a lot of rechecking till your request gets through.

"Go ahead," Mabel said, "I'll stay with it."

The Rutherford phone book listed five Wahlers, but no James. I started calling at the top of the list, with Arthur and Marilyn; Marilyn said there was no James in their household, no James in her family, no James Wahler in town that she knew about.

I called Constance, Joseph, and Ralph, got one no-answer and two denials. I called Tammy. She answered my query with an odd little silence and then asked, "Who's this again?"

"Rutherford Police Department, Ms. Wahler. We're looking for anyone who's acquainted with James Francis Wahler—"

"Why?" she asked, "What's he done?"

"Do you know him, Ms. Wahler?"

"Yeah, I know him. I'm his wife. Ex-wife, I guess you'd say. We been separated for a year, almost. So, has he done something stupid or what?"

"Ms. Wahler, I think it would be better if I came to your home to talk to you. Do you still live at—?" She didn't want me to come there. She wanted to know what was wrong, and she wanted to know it right away, and her anger increased as I evaded her questions. Finally I said firmly, "We'll be there in ten minutes, Ms. Wahler," and hung up quickly, called a squad to take me to her address on Southwest Sixth, and stood in the doorway of her incredibly messy apartment with two big blue uniforms, Casey and Longworth, flanking me. A pale, cross-looking child clung to her leg, sucking a pacifier and whimpering.

Her ex-husband was twenty-three, she said, five-ten, with light brown hair and blue eyes. "Jeez," she said, "hasn't he even got his wallet on him? Musta been one helluva bender. What's he in for, DUI? That schmuck. This one'll cost him his license, and then how's he gonna hold a job? That screwup, he's already two months behind on child support, too."

"Mrs. Wahler," I said, "we have a dead man downtown that we think may be your husband."

You never know. Sometimes the angriest ones care most. The three of us watched her warily; would she cry, scream, have hysterics, faint? Her mouth formed a round "O" and she stood still in the doorway, her eyes going from one face to another. Then she stooped and picked up the fussing child, carried him to the window, and stood looking out.

"Mrs. Wahler," I said gently, "you suppose you could leave your baby with somebody for a few minutes? If you could come downtown with us, you could tell us if this is your husband's body we've got—or not. Think maybe you could do that?"

She turned to stare at me blankly for a moment, then her eyes focused and she said, "Oh, uh . . . yeah. I can drop Donny at my mom's for a few minutes, I guess. Uh . . . you wanna sit down while I . . ." she gestured helplessly toward a couch piled high with laundry, a chair full of toys.

"We'll wait in the car," I said.

She was quiet on the ride downtown, staring out the side window at some reality of her own. In the lab, she stood calmly while the body was wheeled out of the cooler, unmoving while the sheet was pulled back. She looked a long moment at his face, nodded, then reached out to brush back a strand of hair that had fallen over his forehead.

"What happened to him?" she asked softly. "Was he in some kinda accident?"

Longworth looked quickly at me; I shook my head.

"Mrs. Wahler," I said, slipping a hand under her elbow, "do you suppose you could take the time to answer a few questions for me? If we could just sit out here—"

She jerked her arm away from my hand; she was surprisingly strong. "*What happened to him?*" she demanded. Turning back to the table where her husband lay, she peeled the sheet back to his waist, revealing the great Y-shaped incision of the autopsy gaping there. She gasped sharply; the air hit the back of her throat and made her cough. She grabbed the cover as if to hold on, and as she stepped a way from the horror on the table, pulled the covering back to his knees. There was a breathtaking moment of silence while she stared at the wounds where her husband's genitals had been. Then she pressed her hands against the sides of her head and began to scream.

The next half hour seemed long. Tammy Wahler bounced off all four walls of the room we were in, then ran shrieking down the brightly polished center hall of the lab. She crashed through the brass push-bar on the back door and ran out into a small private parking lot, where she began beating and kicking the doctors' cars parked there. Longworth caught her once and tried to hold her in his arms; she broke his glasses and bloodied his nose. I ran and got a lab doctor, who protested that he couldn't give her anything without an examination. But as he spoke, Tammy put all her berserk strength behind one elegant round-house with her purse and broke the hood ornament cleanly off his pearl gray Lamborghini. He ran and filled a syringe and, with three cops helping him, got something into her arm that left her, in a few minutes, limp and sobbing.

We took her back to the house where she had dropped off her baby. Her mother came to the door carrying the whimpering child, took one look at her daughter slumped between Casey and Longworth, and shrieked, "What have you done to my baby?"

Tammy's child cried louder; Tammy began to sob. I had to shout, finally. Over their wails, I yelled that I would call tomorrow and pressed cards from Crime Victims' Services into their unresponsive hands. I bellowed, above the general caterwauling, as much information as I could think of about the many helpful agencies whose services could be coordinated if they would only call this number. Nobody was really listening to me, so I gave up finally and escaped to the squad car.

"I was thinking of trying for a promotion to detective," Tim Casey said on the way downtown, "but hell, it ain't any easier than driving a squad, it is?"

"Man, that's one strong woman," Ted Longworth said, squinting nearsightedly above the Kleenex he had pressed to his nose. Fragments of his ruined eyeglasses were poking his chest through an inside pocket. "You ever see anything like the way she took out the hood ornament on that 'Ghini? Jake?"

"Mmmm." I stared unhappily at gridlocked five-thirty traffic on First Avenue. Having unhappy women yell at me again had sent my emotions ricocheting back into last year's divorce court mode; I felt guilty and ashamed.

"I would say she was surprised, wouldn't you?" I asked them. "When she pulled back that sheet?"

Longworth snorted through his bloody Kleenex. "Yeah, Jake, I'll be glad to testify that the wife had a definite shock reaction."

Back in my office, I found a note on my desk from Mabel Houser, "James Wahler has no arrest records on NCIC." So either James Wahler gave up on crime as a grownup, or he got better at whatever he was doing.

It was five-forty-five, a good time to catch people at home. I got out my lists. But reaching for the phone, I felt the room rotate and realized that fatigue was beginning to swamp me. The back of my tongue ached, and my eyes kept sliding out of focus.

I walked out of the building without speaking to anyone and drove cautiously to a supermarket, feeling disabled. I got chicken and beans at the deli counter, grabbed a six-pack out of the cooler, and drove to my apartment with the scrupulous care and attention of a man walking a tightrope without a net.

While I ate, I watched TV news. Nothing seemed to make any sense except the report of a dead body found in Pioneer Park, and even that sounded vaguely unreal to me. I was thinking about opening a second beer when I fell asleep sitting up.

· FOUR ·

"CHIEF WANTS TO SEE YOU RIGHT AWAY," RUSS SWENSON demanded when I walked in Wednesday morning. Russ thinks his job as morning desk sergeant gives him a license to be an overbearing loud-mouthed arrogant nag, which unfortunately it kind of does.

"Sheesh, lemme get checked in before you yell at me, okay?"

"Hey, take your time, Jake," he said. "McCafferty just said to burn your ass if you weren't in there in ten minutes." He managed to say it so that I knew, beyond any doubt, that he really meant "burn your nigger ass."

"Oh, good," I said, "as long as there's no hurry."

Russ fancies himself a master of the carefully calibrated ethnic slur. Actually, his little asides about fresh watermelon and slaps upside the head are about as subtle as a prostate exam. During my first couple of years in the department, I had recurring daydreams about mushing up his head with a rock. Eventually I reasoned that since I didn't know, myself, which races he might actually be slurring, it was a lot smarter to let his bigotry remain his problem. Now that I've worked all that out with myself, I'm looking for some other excuse to break his face.

I stuck my head in McCafferty's door, saw Les Miller sitting ramrod straight in front of the desk, and began backing out. But McCafferty beckoned, saying, "Come on in, we're just about finished."

He turned back to Miller. "She can run like a goddamn antelope, did you know that? Ran three marathons last year, won second place in one of 'em. You know how long a marathon is? Twenty-six-and-something-goddamn *miles*, Les. Can you run twenty-six miles?"

"Last I heard I wasn't training for no footrace," Les Miller grumbled. "Do your job right, a police officer shouldn't *hafta* run, usually. But she damn well better be able to shoot, Frank, now you know that as well as I do."

McCafferty slapped printouts into a pile in a corner of his desk and said, "Yeah, well, listen. Let's put Harrison with Grass and Frisch with Baumgart. And then you take Win, and see what you can do, spend as much time with her at the firing range as you can. We need to save this recruit if we possibly can, Les, and you're the most experienced field training officer I've got. I think you can do it, and I sure as hell expect you to try." Miller went out looking grouchy, and McCafferty watched his back thoughtfully.

"Three inductees finishing orientation and starting with

FTO's this week. One of them is that Vietnamese girl I told you about, remember? Amy Win."

"I remember you mentioned a Vietnamese recruit," I said, "but I thought you said her name was Un-Goo-Something."

"Yeah, well, I probably did say it like that. It's spelled N-G-U-Y-E-N. But turns out you pronounce it 'Win.' Well, she gets another little sound in there at the beginning that I can't seem to manage, but I said it back to her 'Win,' and she said, 'That's close enough.' Seems like a real straight kid.

"But now Les says she can't shoot for sour apples. Damn disappointing," he fumed, slamming some more printouts around. "You know I got royally racked in St. Paul for not showing enough diversity on the force. Oversight committee said we should be 'reflecting the population' better. I said, 'Shit, I can't hire people that don't apply; and they said, what's that word they used? *Outreach*, we should be doing more *outreach* in the schools. Where the hell do they come up with words like that all of a sudden?

"So now I get an application from this Asian female with great marks in school, got her AA in criminal justice and all her tests indicate motivation up the ying-yang, and she finishes four weeks in Training Division with all reports satisfactory except she can't shoot a gun? What kinda foolishness is that?" He took a long swig of coffee. "Hell, my *aunt Tilly* can shoot a gun."

"Tilly Walsh? You kidding?" I grinned at him. Frank's aunt Tilly brings oatmeal cookies to the department at Christmastime, and little jars of homemade apple butter.

"Damn right. I taught her myself, didn't I ever tell you about that? She got concerned, here a few years ago, when we had that rash of burglaries, that Hench bunch. It was shortly after Uncle Leo died, and I guess she was feeling kind of vulnerable. I tried to talk her out of buying a gun, I was afraid that she'd hurt herself. But then I saw it meant a lot to her to be independent, so I said, 'Okay, I'll teach you myself,' and you know something? She turned out to be a crack marksman. Had a natural aptitude for it. Only she screamed every time she squeezed off a shot, till I said, 'Tilly, you keep screamin' like that, the neighbors are gonna shoot *you*.' And she said, 'Aw, heck, Franny, did I scream?' "

The chief shook his head, grinning. "Anyway! I told Les, I don't wanna hear you tell me that Amy Nguyen can't shoot. I said you been an FTO nine years and you even taught Hisey to use deodorant and quit picking his nose, you can sure as hell teach this intelligent, motivated woman to fire a Glock."

"Les probably ought to take another look at Hisey," I said, "he scratches his crotch and hums now."

"Yeah, well." McCafferty grimaced and switched gears. "So, you had some fireworks when the wife came to identify the body, I hear."

"She was next of kin," I said defensively, "what choice did I have?"

"Did I say you did wrong? Just want you to realize I had several calls already. Her mother and all the neighbor ladies are up in arms about her gettin' shocked like that. And of course the newspaper's been out there, and the TV station's talking to them now, so expect big stories tonight. They've got all the facts on the mutilation now, and they're making the most of it. You got anything besides the ID?"

"Not really, but how about the ID? Got it off the finger-prints the first day, how often does that happen? But listen,

I been wanting to ask you. Whaddaya think, Frank, of the odds of a guy wearing a softball uniform with nothing on underneath?"

"Under one of them stretch suits? You mean no jock-strap or—"

"Or jockey shorts or even a fig leaf, Frank. Exactly. Nothing but skin under that uniform. You ever know anybody to play like that? Also, Frank, this sounds crazy, but Pokey says there's lividity in the bottoms of his feet. Like he stood up after he was dead."

"You're right, it sounds crazy. And playing softball in a stretch uniform with no underwear is out of the question, at least in Rutherford. But then, Jesus, everything about this case is off the wall. What about that picture we found on the body, anything on that yet?"

"No prints. My records search hasn't arrived yet. I want to detail a team to go house-to-house around the park today, see if anybody saw anything, okay?"

"Sure, I told you, all the help you need, just ask."

"Good. Well, I need to make about a thousand phone calls, Frank, so—?"

"Right. Keep me posted."

It was slow going. Nobody on the team lists knew Jim Wahler. Reluctantly, after procrastinating for an hour, I called his wife, who gave me the address of Wahler's one-room efficiency and then suddenly, fiercely, insisted on being present while I searched it.

She brought along her sister, Candy, a big, startling girl in skintight purple Spandex pants, with black-rimmed eyes, brown lipstick, and teased hair. The two stood, thick-limbed and glowering, while the building's owner opened the room.

A couple of pairs of pants and half a dozen frayed shirts hung in the shallow closet, some rancid socks were strewn around the floor. There was no wallet, no money, nothing of any value.

Tammy didn't try to hide her disappointment. She kept turning over the few pitiful relics of her husband's life, looking for salvage. The worthless contents of the room seemed to chafe against the wounds she was already nursing.

"Look at this!" she said, shaking a couple of ratty pairs of boxer shorts at her sister, "nothing but junk!" Candy watched her morosely, clucking sympathetically and shaking her towering hairdo.

I secured the place with a crime scene lock and called in a request for a technician to come out and dust for prints. The owner protested she was already losing the two months' rent that Wahler had owed her, and I promised she could have her property back tomorrow.

"I need to ask you some questions," I told Tammy. "You suppose you and your sister could follow me down to the station?"

"Well . . ." She looked away evasively. "My baby's pretty fussy today, I shouldn't be gone too long."

"I could follow you to your house," I said, "if that would be better."

"This isn't a very good time," she said. "Can't it wait?"

"It'll only take a few minutes," I said, but I could feel her hostility rising, and I didn't want to risk another outburst. Finally I plopped my spiral notebook on top of my car and interviewed her right there on the sidewalk, under her sister's baleful eye.

I didn't get much. Yesterday's hysterics had burned off

the shock of her husband's murder, and whatever lingering affection she might have felt for him seemed to have gone with it. Now she was grimly concentrated on survival for herself and her child. She had leftover grudges about his cheating ways, vague suspicions about who he might have spent her child support money on, but little real knowledge of his habits or whereabouts for the last year. She couldn't come up with the name of a known girlfriend, or even a close male crony.

Her husband, she repeated more than once, had been a screwup. He drank some, smoked a lot of pot, was hell to wake up in the morning. He was chronically late for work and grabbed every excuse to call in sick, so he was often unemployed. When he worked, it was usually in construction trades. She gave me the names of two contractors and a lumberyard.

They had been married three years. Of his record of juvenile crime, she seemed completely ignorant but not very surprised. She denied knowing of any crimes he might have committed since their marriage, though. He had never played softball while she knew him. She could not remember his mother's address, but promised to look it up and phone it to the station.

"If you find any money," she said, regarding me narrowly, "it's legally mine, isn't it?"

"Sure," I shrugged. "We haven't found a wallet, so it's still possible that'll turn up—"

"Uh-huh. Or if one of the companies where he worked had an insurance policy or like that. Or—" her whole thick body began to shake, suddenly, and her face puffed up and got pink and feverish-looking. "It seems like there oughta be *something*—" she protested, sounding choked.

"Mrs. Wahler, did you call the number on the card I left with you yesterday? Do you still have the card? Here"—I gave another one to Candy—"you know, Crime Victims' Services will coordinate other agencies you need for financial help, and medical care for your baby, and—you help her make that call, will you?" I asked her sister, who took the card but glared at it suspiciously. Life had evidently taught Candy to beware of taking paper from strangers.

It was clearly not a good time to ask Tammy the Big Question, but I had to do it before we started down the slippery slope of hysterics again. I took a deep breath and said, "One thing, Mrs. Wahler, I do have to ask you, for the record, where were you Monday night from, say, about nine o'clock till midnight?"

Her head came up, and her brown eyes blazed indignantly through the tears that stood in them. "Me? You want to know where *I* was? I'll tell you where I was, Mr. Smartass, I was home taking care of my baby where I belonged, where that no-good husband of mine has never been since his son was born, that's where I was, and you can ask anybody, ask my Mom, I talked to her on the phone, ask Candy here, she stopped by, because she *knew I'd be alone like he's always left me*, that filthy liar—" Enormous tears spouted out of her eyes; they rolled off her chin and the end of her nose, spattering her blouse. Her voice rose to a keening lament choked with incomprehensible phrases, knots of impotent rage. Tammy was in a lot of trouble. The sonofabitch had died and left her with no place to put her anger.

I wrote, "Mother and sister will support her alibi for the hours surrounding the murder."

Candy put an arm around her and glared at me. "Boy, men are such damn bastards," she said. I stood looking back at her helplessly, not knowing what to say. I closed my notebook and said, "Well, thanks, Mrs. Wahler, if you think of anything else here's my card—"

Neither one of them would take it. They left me standing there like a dork, with my card-holding hand outstretched, while Candy, hugging Tammy close to her, slid into their battered sedan from the passenger's side and drove noisily away on bald tires.

A fat FedEx package was waiting in my office when I got back. I cleared everything else off my desk, switched on the overhead lights, and laid out Trudy Hanson's pictures in rows. I had to get accustomed to the gore and calamity all over again. Crime scenes never seem to photograph quite the way I remember them. In the color shots, the bright lights of the camera rendered the blood-soaked clothes and body in brighter shades than I had ever seen at the park; the victim's face, especially, looked much redder.

There was a second set, of black-and-white glossies. With the sharp highlights and deep shadows that artificial lighting cast, those pictures were shocking in a new way. Black-and-white crime scene photos have an innate sordidness about them, a context they bring with them, I guess, from old tabloid front pages. And the voyeurism of the camera heightened the obscene way Wahler's body had been mutilated and then posed.

I stared at them till my eyes watered, walked to the window and gazed out for a few minutes, went back to my desk and stared again. After ten more minutes I shook my head, gathered the pictures in a pile, went down the hall for a cup of coffee, and came back and scrutinized each picture again under a magnifying glass. In a couple of the black-and-white shots I thought I could see faint ridges that could arguably be the edges of wheel marks near the body. Otherwise there was nothing, factually, in the whole stack that I hadn't noticed before.

But pondering the pictures had changed how I felt about the crime. On Monday night, in the dark, the grotesquely mutilated body had seemed like the work of a madman running amok. Now, looking at the softball bat so carefully posed where the missing genitals had been and the Polaroid picture pinned to the pocket of the suit, I started to believe I was looking at the result of a carefully planned crime, done to make a point. The arrangement of the body wasn't at all accidental, that much was clear. The more I stared at it, the more I thought I could see a message, like a note written in code on the ground. Somebody had used James Wahler's body to say—what?

I was going through them all again with my magnifying glass when Mabel plopped a thick fanfold of flimsy paper in front of me, saying, "Here, Sherlock, hot off the fax."

After a long conversation with a database searcher at BCA, I had requested records of mutilation crimes in Minnesota and the five surrounding states in the last three years. All database searches are composed of a series of frustrating compromises: cast your net too wide, and the search will yield so much it's unwieldy; place too many conditions in your query, and you'll come up almost empty. Computers are wonderful storage bins, but they still don't make intuitive leaps. This search, I saw from the size of the paper stack, had yielded plenty of shocking events. Now, my task would be to eliminate the ones that had no features resembling my case and follow up on the ones that seemed similar.

Putting the pictures aside, I forced myself to read through the whole horrifying list, marking with orange highlighter the few cases that were in any way comparable to the one I was working on. Everything on the list included mutilation, described with devastating accuracy. None concerned softball paraphernalia.

By six-thirty I had a raging headache and a whole new view of the possibilities of depravity. I carried home a small pizza and a large bottle of zinfandel, drank wine in front of the TV set until the picture skewed hopelessly out of focus, and groped my way to bed.

I woke at four A.M. feeling liverish and threatened. I stumbled to the bathroom, peed with my eyes closed, hurried back to bed, and plunged deep under the covers, determined to sleep another two hours. After fifteen minutes of twitching I gave it up and got in the shower. Standing under the hot water, I began composing kinky combinations for BCA to use in an all-states search: try sports equipment/genitalia; photography/sex/softball; how about parks/penises with mutilation/memorabilia?

Squeaky clean but critically low on energy, I drove to an all-night truck stop on the highway and ordered thousands of calories' worth of sausage, fried eggs, muffins, and milk. Except for a couple of burly cross-country movers at the counter and a boothful of hilarious drunks trying to sober up on scrambled eggs, I had the bleak predawn grittiness of the place to myself. It seemed like a good chance to read press accounts of the Jim Wahler murder, so I went outside and got the Rutherford paper from the rack in front.

"Mutilation" seemed a much ruder word on the front page of our normally sedate local newspaper than it did in department records. The picture under the headline was even more shocking, to me; it showed Jim and Tammy together, smiling radiantly. It must have been a wedding or engagement photo, probably the only likeness she had of him. A big, current photo on the lower half of the page showed Tammy holding her sad-looking son. She had put on makeup, and Candy must have helped her with her hair.

The stories occupied almost the entire front page and were substantially correct as far as they went. I was pleased to see there was still no mention of the picture pinned to the uniform. A feature story, under a subhead, about law enforcement efforts in the case included a small picture of Frank talking to reporters. He photographs a little fatter than he is, but it wasn't a bad-looking picture; he was wearing his basic hold-the-fort look. At least they hadn't caught him smiling. Rutherford people watch a lot of TV during the long winters, and like the rest of America they've become concerned lately about the eroding social values they see on the box. As a result they're looking for the gravest decorum in law enforcement personnel, and for judges who hand down maximum sentences. Rutherford citizens are not impressed by Rutherford's low crime rate; they think it should be zero.

At my desk at sunup, feeling keen and virtuous, I got out a new, bright blue, three-ring binder, pasted a neat white label across the spine, and labeled it "Wahler." I turned on my word processor and began transcribing my notes. I wrote the whole story of the investigation in chronological order. Then I broke down the same information into tabbed sections: "Autopsy," "Data Search," "Fingerprints," "Interviews," "Photos." By the time the day shift began coming to work, I had a flattening file of perfectly typed information, organized so I could find everything in it with no hesitation. Unfortunately, I thought as I positioned the blue notebook neatly on the upper left corner of my desk, the whole damn thing adds up to zippo. I was no closer to knowing who killed Jim Wahler, or why, than when I first saw him propped on the ground.

I called St. Paul to put in an early request for a database search and was pleased to find Tom Eckert, my favorite geek, already at his desk. I told him about my "message" hunch. Message killings, Tom said, often involved some aspect of religion gone over the top, a cult thing that had gotten out of hand. Did I want to look for some of those?

"Um. Maybe," I said. "Let me run a couple of other ideas past you before we decide." I gave him the list of queries I'd composed in the shower; he selected a sampling and agreed to try them, as well as cults.

"Am I limiting it too much?" I asked him.

"Believe me," he said, "in an all-states search, this'll be more than you want to read through."

He agreed to forward my request for further information on the three cases I had highlighted off yesterday's list. They were not very similar to my case, but they each had one or two elements in common with mine, and I wanted more information about the victims' clothing and cause of death before I eliminated them completely. In the absence of substantive clues, I was following scanty leads.

Yesterday's interviews of the householders living around the park had yielded one lead. I decided it would save time to combine the follow-up call on that person with interviews of Wahler's employers. Carrying my spiral notebook and list of addresses, I went down and found my car, got in it, and opened all the windows. The temperature card under the clock at the bank said seventy-four degrees. Fat robins were picking worms out of lawns, and a woodpecker was attacking the light pole behind the library. The smell of lilacs hung thick and intoxicating over everything.

Sometimes, on late-May mornings in Rutherford, you can almost hear the grass grow. For a short couple of weeks, the weather probably affects our portion of the gross national product; no matter what you're supposed to be doing, part of you wants to sit still and feel spring happen. The lush fertility of ideal weather, working its magic on six feet of black earth, can simply destroy your determination to rush around being useful. I stretched luxuriously, and made up my mind to go fishing on Sunday without fail.

Dialing up Minnesota Public Radio, I got a classical music program, turned the volume to medium, and drove, without rushing, toward my first address. I don't really know squat about classical music, but I like the sounds. It's one of those things I've decided to learn more about as soon as life slows down a little; it's on the List. Most working Americans have a list like mine, I think; we all intend to read more about the Civil War, or take pottery classes, or learn to tell the major composers apart. One of the women on the night support team is always planning to read the

Russian novelists, and I dated a girl last winter who was making a list of books about Madagascar. She didn't check them out of libraries or buy any of them, just kept a growing list that she intended to read as soon as she got time. I haven't made a whole lot of progress on my own list, so far, but I enjoy adding to it. I figure it's going to be a better retirement project than building birdhouses in the garage.

Neil's Lumber had changed hands since Jim Wahler worked there, and the old records were gone with the previous owner. A sweetly smiling red-haired girl ran the office for the new owner; she wore one of those loose cotton sleeveless shifts that show another cotton garment, like a sports bra, underneath. Her pale, round arms emerged from their wonderland of double cotton, like the right answer to a question I hadn't realized I'd been asking. I watched the thin gold chain she wore around her neck move with the pulse in her throat while I asked her many careful questions about where those pesky old records might have gone. By the time we concluded she was not going to be able to help me, she had already helped me so much that I was only just able to get the door open, and I left the lumberyard aglow with youth and vigor.

The next two names were small contractors who had to be traced to their job sites, following sparse clues to poorly marked locations. On a different day it might have been a nightmare job, but in this perfect weather it was like a delightful paper chase, with quirky directions and large, interesting machines for added ploys.

I went after Schutt Concrete Products first. Mrs. Schutt ran the office out of a lean-to off their kitchen; she said her husband was installing a section of new sewer line in a development on the far north side. Her directions were pretty straightforward, and I followed them correctly as far as the turnoff onto graveled county road. I guessed wrong, though, about which of two muddy tracks to follow off-road, and created a new ditching system when I had to back out of an empty field that was well on its way to being a swamp. My second guess was better. It led to a painted sign that told me this would soon be the subdivision of Lynn-wood, where I would be able to buy three bedrooms, two baths, starting at eighty-nine nine. Across a moonscape of heaped earth and mud-holes, I spied a crew making the mess bigger.

I carry boots in the back of the car for these occasions. I put them on and hiked across the wrecked hay field. Across a fence, in a pasture where horses still grazed, a meadow-lark was singing.

The first man I found leaned down from shoveling sand into a cement mixer to listen to my request and identified the man on the backhoe as Ole Schutt. I strode to the edge of the hole Schutt was digging, screamed hello, and held up my badge. He couldn't hear a word I said. He squinted down at my wallet, reading all the information on it twice, occasionally looking dubiously from the photo to my face. Finally he shut off his backhoe and climbed down reluctantly, all his body language making it plain he was a man with a schedule to keep. I showed him my badge again and explained my mission.

"Oh, yeah, I saw the story in the paper last night. Damn shame, young fella like that, with a little kid and all. Some freako just up and killed him, huh?"

"Well, we don't know who killed him yet, Mr. Schutt," I said. "That's what I'm trying to find out, that's why I'm talking to everybody I can find who knew him."

"Yeah, well, just forget the mister stuff, call me Ole, okay? Good enough for these numskulls"—he waved an arm at his crew—"oughta be good enough for you. Yeah, Jim worked for me, oh, hell, guess it musta been a coupla years off and on. Depends on the work, y'know, I can't keep everybody on full-time."

"Did he play on a softball team while he worked for you?"

"Softball?" He looked nonplussed and annoyed; was I going to take up his time with nonsense questions? Then he remembered and said, "Oh, yeah, that's right, you found him on one of the softball fields in the park, didn't you? No, I never knew him to play on a team. But then I didn't know him in a personal way, you understand—he just worked for me now and then."

I sensed a reticence in his answer; Ole Schutt was trying not to speak ill of the dead.

"How would you rate him as an employee?" I asked.

Ole Schutt took off his hard hat and scratched his head, stared into a ditch for a minute, then shrugged and said, "Oh, Jim was okay as long as you kept your eye on him. He was just . . . kind of a doofus, y'know? He showed up late a lot. Oh, hell—" He shrugged again helplessly. "You want the truth, right? I finally fired the guy. He didn't do anything *bad*, really, he was just so damn lazy and aimless. I finally got sick of it and got somebody to replace him."

"He have any enemies that you know of?"

"*Enemies?* Jim Wahler?" Schutt stared in disbelief. "No.

Why would he have enemies? Nobody even took him seriously. Hell, he was just a"—he wobbled his hands helplessly—"just a *slob*."

I got a hamburger at the next fast-food place I came to and went looking for Barber's Roofing, where Wahler had worked last. It was a tiny shop on Highway 52 South, in a dilapidated building that also housed a septic-tank cleaning company and a shop that sold lawn sprinklers. I almost missed it because it was set back from the road, inconspicuous between a big farm implement store and Harvey's Feed & Seed.

The door stood open. I walked through into a small, cluttered space. A rough worktable, made of sawhorses and planks, occupied the center of the room, dimly lit by a hanging fluorescent fixture with one burned-out bulb. One wall was lined with shelves holding rolls of felt paper, staple guns, and blocks of tar wrapped in brown paper. There was a big iron kettle and half a dozen mops against the opposite wall.

A voice was audible somewhere in back. I followed a sort of path through the clutter to a windowless two-by-four office, where cigarette smoke hung in a foul-smelling pall. A thin, pale boy of fifteen or so was perched on a corner of the desk, smoking and talking on the phone. There was nothing on the desk but a spindle with a couple of bills impaled on it and a dog-eared order pad. There was no chair in the room. A big calendar featuring costumed chimpanzees doing humanoid tasks hung on the wall beneath him.

The kid jumped off the desk when he saw me, said, "Hang

on a sec," into the phone, and pressed the mouthpiece against his skinny chest. "Help ya?" He asked me.

"I'm looking for A. J. Barber," I said.

"Ace is out on a job," he said. "Can I help ya? You need to see him about a roof repair? I can take a message," he suggested hopefully. I almost left one; I could see he wanted to practice his secretarial skills. But the shop suggested that A. J. Barber might not return calls promptly.

"I really need to talk to him in person," I said, "just for a minute or two." I smiled my most harmless smile. "How about telling me where he's working?"

"Well—sure. Guess that's okay." He muttered into the phone, "Call you back, okay?" and hung it up. He turned back to me and said, "You know where Cramer's Body Shop is? That's whose roof he's doing, Cramer's."

"West side of town? Out near the water tower?"

"Yup."

"Yeah, I can find it. Thanks."

I got back in the car, guiltily pleased to learn I had another long drive ahead of me. Cramer's Body Shop is on a short street next to Fork Creek, on the extreme west edge of Rutherford, where town and country merge. It's an area of small ma-and-pa shops interspersed with clusters of houses, with here and there a potato patch, a cornfield, or a barn full of horses.

I dawdled along, always going west toward the right neighborhood but not necessarily by the shortest route, turning whenever a street dead-ended at the creek. Chopin trilled out of my speakers; I knew it was Chopin because I caught the announcement at the beginning of the piece. I think maybe I'll recognize that one the next time I hear it;

piano that makes you think of Mary Lou Retton doing back flips off the high beam.

The neighborhoods got more marginal and disorganized as I approached the edge of town. A very young mother in a big T-shirt and curlers walked her toddler patiently along a cracked sidewalk, singing softly down at him as he staggered bravely along on bowed legs. A couple of jays screamed in the willows overhanging the stream. I could see the reflections of willow branches in the slow-moving water, with the fat white cumulus clouds towering above, and my bones urged me to stretch out on the grass by the riverbank and let law enforcement take care of itself for an hour.

But a distinct inner vision had begun traveling around with me, of Frank, sitting erect and proper at his desk, reading a copy of this morning's *Rutherford Post-Intelligencer*. He had just reached the last line of the story, which read, "The police, as yet, have no clues to the identity of the murderer." Frank's face, as he read it, wore the expression of a man trying to swallow a frog.

So I put aside my springtime urge to dawdle and drove steadily toward Cramer's Body Shop. I parked in front, alongside a beat-up blue pickup, speckled all over with tar and paint. It had six big tar barrels in back and a sign on the driver's-side door: Barber's Roofing. Under the name was a streak of blue body paint that did not quite match the truck. Faintly, through the paint, as I went by, I could read a street address and phone number in Fort Dodge, Iowa.

Mrs. Cramer, a brown-eyed matron whose sweet smile and glorious bosom disguised a flawless memory and dazzling math skills, was running the store as usual. She directed me to the left rear of the building, where she predicted I would find a ladder. I climbed it to the roofline, looked over the drainpipe, and found two men hard at work. The one near me was spreading hot tar with a mop. He looked up and met my eyes. I asked him, "You A. J. Barber?"

He shook his head and pointed across the roof, where a man on his knees was stapling felt paper. He shouted across, "Ace?" When Barber looked up, the mop man pointed at my head and said, "Man wants to talk to you." Barber got up off his rubber knee pads and came over.

I held up my badge and asked, "Got a minute to talk to me?"

Barber was a thin man with a pronounced overbite, freckled all over his face and arms; he had sparse curly hair that must have been red once but now was faded rusty tan. He was probably not much over forty, but outdoor work had wrinkled him, making deep squint marks around his narrow, pale blue eyes. He reacted to the sight of my badge like a man meeting a rattlesnake in tall grass.

"I got nothing to say to you! I don't want no trouble with the law! I do my job and pay my taxes, and you busybodies oughta leave me alone!" he shouted.

It's happened to me before. People don't live their lives in suspension, after all, waiting for the magic day when Jake Hines comes to call on them. They have protocols, agendas, pissing matches, going on that I know nothing about. When I find I have landed, all unawares, in the middle of somebody's personal tornado, I adopt a firm, schoolteachery manner and deepen my voice a couple of notches. Sometimes it works.

"Mr. Barber," I intoned, in the most righteous tones I could summon, "I need to talk to you about James Wahler."

"I told that dyke from social services in Fort Dodge that I—" The momentum of his temper tantrum carried him that far before he could hear me. Then my words began to penetrate his narrow brain pan. He executed a classic double take, like Wile E. Coyote deciding in midfall to go back to the top of the cliff. His eyes refocused and met mine, and he said, "Who?"

"James Wahler. The man who was found dead in the park Sunday night. His wife says you were his last employer."

"Wahler. James Wah—oohhh, Jimmy!" It was fun watching him switch gears, becoming your average jovial working stiff on a roof. "Oh, yeah—Jimmy worked for me sometimes. And he was working for me when he got killed, I guess. I *guess* he was still working for me—" He laughed, a short humorless bark. "I was so mad at him all day Tuesday for not showing up, I made up my mind, no two ways about it, I said this time I'm gonna fire that guy. Then I looked at the paper, when I got home that night, and I saw the poor bastard got hisself killed." The little bark sounded again. "Kinda took the wind outta my sails, know what I'm sayin'?"

"Can you tell me a little bit about him, Mr. Barber?"

"Hey, call me Ace, will ya? Mr. Barber's my grampaw. Whaddaya say, let's climb down offa here and have a smoke, huh?" I watched his lean shanks come down the ladder behind me. On the ground he appeared frailer, almost critically thin, and shorter than I thought. He fished in an inside shirt pocket, pulled out a pack of cigarettes, offered me one. I shook my head, and he leaned into the lighter flame, sucked smoke into his lungs gratefully, and asked, "So, whaddaya wanna know?"

"Did he work for you long? Was he a good employee?"

"No and no. After the first couple of jobs he did for me, three, four months ago, I seen he was one of them guys that get the work out fairly well as long as you're right there lookin' at them, and otherwise they mostly goof off. After that I only called him in when I couldn't find nobody else."

"Ever see him away from work?"

"Jimmy? You kiddin'? Time you put up with bad news like him all day, not likely you're gonna wanna see him after."

"Ever know him to play softball? Play on a team?"

"Softball?" He looked at me as if I must be a little daft. "Shit, all he thought about was livin' from one joint to the next. He was so fulla dope he couldn't even get up in the morning, half the time. Who would want him on a team?"

"Did he have any friends that you remember?"

"Nah. But he could have a whole clubhouse fulla buddies and I wouldn't know 'em. I didn't wanna have anything to do with the guy, never talked to him except about the job. Hard enough to get him to pay attention to that much."

I was closing my notebook when I thought of one last thing. "So, did Wahler have any pay coming, Ace?"

"Um—" He looked over my shoulder and pretended to think about it. His lack of good intentions was so transparent I almost laughed. I wrote Tammy's address on a sheet of my notebook, tore it out, and handed it to him. "Here's the widow's name and address. Will you send it to her, whatever you owe him? She's pretty hard up, and there's a little boy."

"You bet," he said, folding the sheet of paper several times before tucking it in beside his cigarettes, "I'll look it up tonight."

Try small claims court, Tammy, I thought as I turned to walk away. From behind me, Ace Barber's hard, dry laugh sounded again. "Say, I'm sorry about that big speech I made when you first got here. What kinda threw me off, you know," he said, "is you don't look like no ordinary cop. Where you from, anyways?" he asked as I turned back. He stood looking skinny and taut, a fake smile showing through his sunburned freckles.

I'd forgotten the temper tantrum he threw when I arrived. If he hadn't brought it up, I'd never have thought about it again. While we were talking, he had seemed like a typical small entrepreneur, tense and harried, taking a flyer on short cash and irritated by trifling malingerers. Now, from two paces away, I got a sense that Ace Barber had some extra worries. Trying to blame his outburst on the color of my skin made no sense; he had reacted to my badge, not my face.

"Hey, no problem," I said, in my deacon's voice. I waved my notebook like a benediction, ignoring his question about my place of birth. He stood and watched me as I got back in my car and started it; I gave him another jaunty little wave as I backed out of the parking space. He raised one hand, like Chief Joseph of the Nez Percé, and stood like that, watching me thoughtfully till I was back on the highway. As soon as I was out of sight, I called in the license number of his truck. I had not been looking for anything in particular from Ace Barber, and he had not given me anything, in direct answers to my questions, that I hadn't heard before. But his combination of mendacity and unease rang all the bells on my Phony Meter, so I bagged my last inter-

view and went back to the station to run him through all
existing records.

Nothing came back on the truck, but I found an out-
standing warrant for his arrest, in Iowa. On a hunch, I went
on and found two more warrants, older, in Illinois and
Michigan. Ace Barber was a deadbeat dad. His wife was a
determined lady who had been on his case for years. Every
time she got close, he skipped again, and she started over.
Ace Barber was not buying the oatmeal for his three sons in
Kalamazoo.

I sent a teletype to Des Moines. They sent one back, veri-
fying that the warrant was still active. I tucked it in the inside pocket of my jacket and called for a marked squad car
to take me to Cramer's Body Shop. I got Miller and Nguyen.
Les said Amy hadn't done an arrest based on a warrant
yet, so she might as well get in on this one. Like all hard-
working FTOs, Les monitors radio traffic carefully and
negotiates for the calls that will give his trainees the range
of experience they'll need after they leave him. He and
Frank have worked out a point system for everything from
paperwork through rough trade; trainees don't get cut
loose till their score says they're ready.

Amy Nguyen drove, under Les's direction, smoothly exe-
cuting his suggestions for the quickest route and listening
meekly when he criticized her technique at a four-way stop.
Taking guff about my driving was one of the hardest things
in the training course, for me. Frank was a stickler for by-
the-book procedures, and his constant hectoring distracted
me so I could hardly operate the car at all. I got stuck in a
snowbank once, after Frank unexpectedly said, "Pull over
here and park." We had to call for a tow. Frank said, "I

meant pull over where it's shoveled," and then sat and glared straight ahead, never saying another word, while we waited half an hour for the truck. I almost gagged. It was the closest I ever came to quitting the force. Watching Amy Nguyen now, quietly taking directions, outwardly impervious to the embarrassment she had to be feeling, I was impressed by her cool.

By the second or third day of a recruit's time with an FTO, they're becoming friends or they're being elaborately polite to hide the fact that they can't stand each other. Miller, I could see, had Nguyen firmly under his wing and was pleased with his baby chick. Nguyen tolerated his fussing gracefully, soaking up information as fast as he could pour it into her tiny right ear. She looked so damn cute in that blue uniform, it was hard to take her seriously. That, I thought, was probably going to be her biggest problem. She might have to get extra tough with people to keep them from treating her like some kind of adorable toy cop.

I watched her eyes in the rearview mirror, trying to decide whether their shape looked a little like mine. At one time in my childhood, my caseworkers favored Asian for my ethnic description, but when my nose began to grow they gave it up. Amy began to get nervous, thinking I was flirting with her, so I busied myself with my notes.

The roofing truck was gone from Cramer's.

"He left right after you did," Mrs. Cramer told me. "Said something had come up, he'd have to come back and finish the job tomorrow." She shook her head impatiently. "I was pretty disgusted. He promised they'd get done today. I don't like having that mess around any longer'n I have to. People don't like it."

We hustled right over to Barber's place, but we were too late. His shop and apartment stood unlocked and empty. Whatever clothes and equipment had ever been there were gone. Ace Barber, in his speckled pickup, had sped away toward roofs unknown.

There were a couple of pieces of junk mail, addressed to Boxholder, in the wastebasket at the apartment. I took them along, for prints.

We went back to the station and put out an APB, but I knew that the chances of catching Barber were not great. Deadbeat dads, for some reason, get more adept than most petty crooks at staying ahead of the warrant, and Ace Barber had been running for some time, so he knew all the tricks. He probably had three or four license plates for that truck, and a couple of off-road hideaways spotted in every neighborhood. Also, it was nearly five o'clock. The law never sleeps, of course, but it gets noticeably more sluggish out of office hours. If Ace Barber could stay out of sight for one more day, till the weekend, he was probably good for a fresh start in another state.

His skipping right now pretty much forced me to list him as a suspect for my crime, too. It was possible that Jim Wahler had learned about Barber's warrant skips and made some half-assed attempt to blackmail him. It would have been a dumb idea, certainly, but given Wahler's track record as a jerk, it was possible. Still, supposing Barber killed Wahler to shut him up, why would Barber do all that funny business, the mutilation and the posing? What possible reason could he have to dress him in a softball uniform and pin a picture on his shirt? That didn't make any sense. Unless—

Who said a deadbeat dad couldn't also be a kinky serial killer? It was too late to get my records man back today, but I made a note to get him to search Illinois, Michigan, and Iowa for mutilation crimes that might coincide with Barber's times in those states. I took the two letters I'd found in the trash back to the evidence room and turned them in, with a request for prints.

Jimmy Chang's report was waiting on my desk. Jim Wahler's blood showed .02 level of alcohol, well below intoxication. He did test positive for marijuana. That was no surprise. There was no trace of other drugs, or poison. He had nothing under his fingernails but dirt. His stomach contained partially digested food "consistent with five or six hours of processing."

I called Pokey's office. His receptionist said he was with a patient but almost finished. "Ask him to call me," I said, and he did, in three minutes.

"Have you read Jimmy Chang's report?"

"Yah. Two, three times."

"Okay, you see anything here that changes anything?"

"Sure don't. Guy didn't die from smokin' dope. I'm gonna put down death by strangulation, by jeepers."

"Okay. And you agree it could have been done with the cable from the gate padlock?"

"Yup. Or one like it. Or some kinda wire like that."

"Okay, one more thing. You still gonna say there was lividity in the soles of the feet?"

"Gotta say it, Jake. It was there."

"Meaning my man got up and walked around—"

"Not walked. Stood. Was stood up by somebody."

"Like, to move him, you think?"

"Hey, I don't hafta know for what. I just tell about lividity in feet to my smart cop friends and they figger out why is." Pokey's voice took on a conspiratorial tone and he chuckled delightedly. "But listen, Jake, you gotta tell me. That dead man's wife, she beat up on you and two blue uniforms and rich lab doctor besides? That sweet girl in paper with baby?"

"Go squeeze a pimple, Pokey," I said.

I had one name left on my list of people to see today: Anne Condon, the woman my door-to-door teams had found. It was too late to bother her now. I put her name at the top of tomorrow's calendar and drove home through the sweet-smelling dusk.

Maybe my landlord would let me plant a row of tomato plants in the backyard by the garage, I thought. I could trade him some hedge work. I knew I could do a better job with corners than the guy who was trimming for him now. I left a message on his answering machine and fell asleep thinking about fertilizer.

· FIVE ·

MY POSTDIVORCE PAD IS IN A BEAT-UP BLOCK OF FUR-
nished apartments, wedged between a highway and a row
of saloons. The usual noise level runs somewhere between
a neighborhood brawl and a five-car pileup, so my brain
no longer responds to ordinary nighttime clamor. But the
clever devils who empty those big commercial Dumpsters
at five in the morning find ways to vary both the sound
level and the duration of their attack. On Friday at dawn, the
Rutherford Solid Waste System driver executed a double-
crash connect, followed by a stupendous triple emptying
shake (clang-a-clang-a-clang-a), that made me sit up in bed
and ask the floor lamp, "What?"

I couldn't get back to sleep, so by chance I was in my car,
showered and dressed, at ten minutes to six, listening to Ed
Gray's voice on the radio. He was calling for any car in sec-

tion eight to see the man in running shorts at Sixty-third Avenue and Green Street Northwest. Cooper and Maddox answered the call.

Being wide awake hours before my shift, listening to other people work, lent a luxurious edge of a fragrant, shiny morning. I left the radio on and drove a couple of blocks aimlessly, debating breakfast choices: bacon and eggs at a truck stop, or juice and a bagel at the new vegetarian restaurant downtown. My one previous experience in a vegetarian place had felt like taking Communion; bits of tasteless food, reverently served on spotless doilies by scrubbed females with the rapt, ecstatic expressions of young nuns. If my body was a temple, why was its occupant craving grease and salt? Shrugging off the guilt, I was pulling into the truck stop when Cooper called in for help.

"We got a man here, very upset, somebody's gonna hafta help him, get him to a counselor, I think, or maybe a hospital. And I need another car, Ed, to help me secure this crime scene, and you better call Jake Hines, we got another DOA with a—I don't want to talk about it on the radio, okay? Just get Jake over here."

I picked up my microphone and said, "Buzz, this is Jake, where are you exactly?"

"I'm in Willow Creek Park. The little park with the wooden jungle gym, between Green Street and Willow Creek, Jake. I'm on the only softball diamond in the park, with a . . . We got another kinky one, buddy."

Ed cut in. "All right, you're on your way then, Jake, right? And you still think you need another car, Buzz?"

"Definitely. This is a busy neighborhood, I see school bus stops on two corners of this block. We're gonna have school kids running all over here in an hour and a half, and there's no fence on this park. I'm very concerned about crowd control."

"Copy," Ed said. "We'll be changing shifts here in a few minutes, but . . . I'll stay on this with you, Buzz. You can hang on out there for a couple hours?"

"Copy. Better have somebody call my wife, I won't have time. Maddox's wife too."

I cut in. "Ed, this is Jake. Could you have the coroner called, too, and BCA? And I guess the chief would want to know, huh?"

"Copy. We'll take care of it." I could picture the explosion of work that would start at the station two seconds after Gray ended his transmission. If there's ever an Olympic event called Task Allocation, Ed Gray will be a contender. His concentration is awesome; he spews out a steady stream of precise orders, without pausing for breath, making tiny check marks on a list that's illegible to everybody but him. His voice, always commanding, rises under stress to an unbearable stentorian shout. His support team does the work right away to get him to shut up.

The quiet morning streets were almost empty. I poured on speed and beat the second squad car to Willow Creek Park; it rounded the corner at the light while I parked in the middle of the block on Green Street. Maddox was sitting on a bench near the sidewalk, with his arm around the shoulders of a slender man in nylon shorts, who was weeping. A small, furry dog, fastened to the bench by his leash, lay quietly at their feet with his head on his paws. Cooper stood a few yards away, by the backstop of a softball diamond, where a fourth man rested on his haunches in a ballplayer's uniform, wearing a catcher's chest protector and face mask.

Maddox met my eyes over the head of the distressed man in his embrace. He continued to talk to him softly while pointing silently toward Cooper with his free hand. I walked toward Buzz Cooper and his squatting companion, whose catcher's mitt, I now saw, was lying on the ground at his feet. He was hunkered in the classic pose of the softball catcher, back of home plate but a little behind the usual position.

Actually, I realized as I got closer, the catcher's rump was propped against the wooden backstop. His left arm hung down to the ground, as though to support his squat, but it wasn't holding him up; it hung limp and useless, with the fingers curled slightly inward just above the dirt. His right arm lay across his knee, pointing toward second base. His right hand was missing.

It had been chopped off crudely at the wrist. Blood had dripped from the stump onto the ground, spattering his shoes and the leather mitt that lay near his feet. His wrist was still oozing a little blood, through the clots that had formed and blackened over the wound. He appeared to be otherwise unhurt.

He was a pudgy young man with longish dark hair, curling just above his shoulders. A roll of fat bulged over the top of his tight-stretched pants. His cheeks were bright red. His neck was too deeply buried in its double roll of fat for me to get a look at it. I leaned over him, smelling blood, sweat, beer, and something else—not mothballs, but a stale storage smell, coming from his suit. It had been stored a long time in a dusty place, in a plastic sack. The same smell had hung on Wahler, I remembered, when we first found him.

I touched his neck, behind the ear; it was cool, and there was no pulse. The fingers of his left hand were getting stiff. His eyes were fixed. Flies clustered at his mouth and nose.

The front pocket of his blouse was plain, with no name embroidered on it. A frontal Polaroid shot of him, posed just as he was now, was pinned to the pocket.

"Look behind the mask," Cooper said, in a strangled voice. I pulled on plastic gloves and gently lifted the mask away from the catcher's face. I dropped it almost at once and said, "Oh, Christ."

A penis and two hairy balls were stuffed down the victim's throat. I looked to see if they were his own. His position made it easy to see that they were not. His own were so evident, in fact, that I did a quick peek down his waistband and confirmed my immediate hunch: this ballplayer wasn't wearing any underwear either.

I made myself look under the mask again. The tormented flesh crammed into the victim's face was not oozing blood like his wrist. It had old, dried blood caked on it, where it had been crudely cut out of some other body, some time ago.

I dropped the mask and asked Cooper, "The man who's crying, he's the one who called in?"

"Yes. Creed, his name is, Jerry Creed. He was waiting for us by the phone booth, over there on the corner. He says he often cuts through this park on his morning run, he likes the gravel paths and the shade. Always brings his dog along. This morning his dog saw the man kneeling here and ran over to him. He started licking something on the ground and wouldn't come back when he was called.

"Creed came over to get his dog, and . . . when the ball-player didn't move, or say anything, for some reason he, Creed I mean, he reached out and touched the glove. The glove was still on the hand then, see? Arm, I mean. So the jogger touched it, poor fella, and it fell off on the ground. And I suppose it looked to him as if he'd just knocked the man's hand off, or like the guy was just . . . falling apart. Must have been like living your worst nightmare. But you can see, the hand is missing. The mitt's got nothing in it but blood. The hand doesn't seem to be anywhere around here."

Cooper paused for a ragged breath. He had not looked at me since I arrived, and he was not meeting my eyes now. Observing the gross physical insults inflicted on the victim had filled him with nameless, puzzling guilt, I could see; his voice sounded defensive, and his eyes darted past my shoulder, making him look like a kid caught in the jam jar. The muscles of his face were stiff, and a nerve twitched in his jaw.

"Best I can tell, Creed never even looked behind the mask. Good thing, I guess. He did all the right things, actually, got a leash on his dog and ran to the phone and called us. He was still okay when we got here, too, but while he was telling us about it, he just seemed to . . . *crumble*. . . . Boy, Maddox was good with him, you know that? I didn't know what to do, but Clint just turned into a big daddy and started taking care of the guy."

Cooper's set white face was regaining its normal agreeable lines as he talked. Waiting alone by the body had frazzled his nerves; now he was having a gregarious reaction. He asked me, "This looks like the same MO as the case you've been working on, doesn't it?" and I could see he was hoping for a gabfest. I wanted to oblige him, but I already had that awful feeling of urgency, too many tasks and not enough time. I held up a hand, said "Hang on a minute," and bolted for my car. I grabbed the microphone and called the station, got the day dispatcher, Cunningham, and asked him, "Gray still there?" When Gray came on the line, I asked him, "Ed, do you think that BCA van's on its way yet?"

"No, and unfortunately they say there's likely to be a delay of several hours today, Jake. Guess they had quite a crime spree in the Cities last night."

"Okay, I want to you call 'em back, please, and tell 'em that we definitely, definitely are gonna need a DNA workup done here. If they give you any heat, tell 'em I'll give 'em all the written justification they need just as soon as I get back to my desk. I'm gonna need DNA done on this victim, Ed, and on my previous victim as well. Two kits, for sure, tell 'em. Okay, Ed?"

DNA tests are expensive. The state of Minnesota does not do one on a whim. Requests for DNA workups are hedged behind enough paperwork to discourage all but the most urgent petitioners.

"You got it, Jake," Ed said. Rounding up toward nine hours of a killer shift, he just kept getting more composed. He thrives on nights that drive everybody else nuts.

"Oh, and listen, one more thing. Will you call the Hampstead County Pathology Lab, please? And tell them, number one, we'll be bringing a body there for autopsy shortly, and number two, under no circumstances are they to release Jim Wahler's body until I say so. Can you do that right away, Ed?"

"Copy," Ed said, "BCA for DNA, county lab for autopsy, and a hold on Wahler's body. Anything else?"

"Call me if there's any problem about those DNA tests, will you? I gotta have 'em."

"Copy," Lieutenant Gray said, dryly. He thinks younger cops get too involved with bells and whistles. He told me once, "Believe it or not, we used to put crooks in jail before we *had* cell phones."

I saw the chief getting out of his car, and Pokey parking right behind him. The chief stopped to say a word to the second squad. It was Greeley and Mundt, I saw as I walked toward them. I looked at my watch. Six-thirty. We were still pulling crews off the night shift.

"Guess we'll need the scene taped off," Frank told them. "Make a big circle around it, will you, and then start patrolling the perimeter to keep curiosity seekers away. Should be some help out here for you soon. Sure appreciate you staying on to help."

As I walked up to Frank, he asked me quickly, "Is there a picture on this one too?"

"Yep. Wait'll you see what else."

After Pokey and Frank had both had a first look around, I told them, "Look under the mask," and raised it with my gloved hands.

The difference in their reactions was interesting. Frank swore and looked sick, as I had. He was appalled, almost to tears; his eyes got a watery, bright look, and the end of his nose got red.

Pokey nodded once and said, softly, "Ah, yah." He looked sad and, momentarily, old.

"This is what I was afraid of as soon as I saw that first picture," Frank said. "More killing and more dirty tricks. We got a kinkster here who's playing games with us, Jake. We gotta find the sonofabitch and put a stop to it!"

"I don't think it's any game, Frank," I said. I told him about my message hunch. He treated me to ten seconds of his blue-laser stare. "You mean this killer is trying to tell us something? This is a puzzle and we're supposed to figure it out?"

"I'm saying he's telling somebody something. The message may not be for us."

Frank shook his head impatiently like a man shooing flies, and said, "I dunno, Jake. That's too deep for me."

Greely and Mundt had started around us with the crime scene tape, using existing trees and posts where they could and sticking posts in the ground where they needed them. Greely kept glancing over at the victim, and I heard him ask his partner something sharply. He dropped the tape suddenly and came over.

"Hey, Jake? Listen, I think I know this guy. Can I—?" He gestured toward the mask.

"I'll do it," I said. "Get ready, Vince, it's not pleasant."

"Wait a minute. Mundt? C'mon over here. If this is who I think, Harley knows him too."

I lifted the mask. Greeley screwed his face up, then squinted and shook his head. Mundt made a sound, like gagging, and turned his back to us.

"Sure enough," Vince said. "It's Frenchy LaPlante. Don't you know him, Jake? He's a big sports fan, always at all the games, and around at the bars after games. Any games, softball, basketball, hockey, he's a fan. Was, I mean. Lotta times he'd buy a round of drinks for the players so he could sit with 'em and get in on the postmortems." He looked some more. "What's he doin' in the uniform, I wonder? I never knew him to play." He turned to his partner. "You ever know Frenchy to play on a team, Harley?"

Mundt half-turned back toward his partner and mumbled something indistinct. Greeley grinned, pounded Mundt's shoulder, and said, "Hey, you okay, buddy?" He winked at Frank and me and said, "We better finish with the tape. We'll be right here if you want any more from us, Jake."

"Wait," I said. "You know who'd be next of kin?"

They looked at each other. "He's not married, I'm pretty sure," Vince said. "He still live at home, do you know?" he asked Harley. Harley shrugged. "Trying to think of his father's name," Vince said. "Lessee—Louie, Louis? No, that's *his* name. His Dad's is Fred? No—"

"Ferdy," Harley Mundt said.

"Right! That's it, Ferdy LaPlante, works on the maintenance crew at the downtown Hilton, last I knew."

I wrote it down. "Thanks. I'll get back to you," I said, and trotted toward the bench, where Maddox was tenderly urging his still-shaking runner to his feet. A van from Methodist Hospital waited at the curb. A white-suited ward tech was taking over care of Jerry Creed, while a social worker quietly questioned Maddox. I remembered her from a domestic abuse case, Erica somebody. Iron hand in an iron glove, I thought when I first encountered her. Confident voice, icy eyes, steely composure. Hey, maybe she's Mother Teresa in deep disguise; my childhood left me unable to relate well to social workers.

Maddox appeared to split down the middle for half a minute, patting and murmuring encouragement to his patient while making the handoff with his left side, the right side of his face and head responding to Erica's questions.

"—tough enough to find a dead guy first thing in the morning," I heard him explaining, "but when he touched the body and the hand fell off, looks like it shook him up pretty bad."

Erica made notes in a tiny leather-covered notebook, her glance flicking repeatedly from Maddox to the weeping man. When she'd heard enough she said abruptly, in the middle of one of Maddox's sentences, "Thanks, Officer," and shook his hand. She had already started around the van to the driver's side when I got there; I tagged her footsteps like a pesky kid, telling her who I was and why I needed time with her patient.

She slid behind the wheel, told me firmly that her first priority was getting this man to the hospital and evaluating his condition, and started the motor before I could argue. She handed out her card and said I might, *if I wished*, call her in a couple of hours. She bullied her way into traffic and left while I was still putting together a sentence about where I *wished* she would put her attitude.

Just as well, too. She had my witness. For a while, all roads to Jerry Creed would lead through Erica. Wasn't that a fun thought? I clipped her card inside my notebook and went back to my car.

The phone book listed three LaPlantes: Alfred, Constance, and Ferdinand. No listing for Louis. I dialed Ferdinand. After the fifth ring, a female voice said "Hell-lo?" in a voice that sounded as if it might be coming from the bottom of a well.

"Does Louis LaPlante live at this address?"

"Yeah." Her breathing was labored; she wheezed.

"Could I speak to him, please?" You never know. There could be a live Louie as well as a dead one.

She coughed. "Who is this?" she finally managed, in a strangled voice.

I identified myself, trying to sound severe. The woman seemed immovable. She wheezed a few more times while she digested the information, then said petulantly, "Just a minute," and set the phone down so that it bounced several times, punishing my ear. From a distance, I heard her call, "Ferd?" and get a short, sharp retort from someplace farther away. There was a long, shouted conversation, perhaps between the back door and the yard, or the kitchen and the basement. Finally hard, quick footsteps came toward the phone, and a man's voice, loud and impatient, said, "Yeah?"

I went through the whole identification rigmarole again. Ferdy LaPlante heard me out, then said flatly, "My son ain't here, mister."

"Do you know where I can reach him?"

Again that silence, then, "What is this?" he asked, getting angry. "Whaddaya want callin' me up this time of the morning?"

I was afraid he was going to hang up. I said, "Mr. La-Plante, I have a young male here, found dead in the park about an hour ago, and two people have identified him as Louis, or Frenchy, LaPlante. Now, if you have a son by that name, and you know where he is, I'd appreciate your saying so, and I won't need to bother you any more."

There was another silence, then his voice, a few feet from the phone, asked, "Francine? Louie say where he was going last night?" Some muttering followed. He came back to me and said, "Our son lives here, mister, but he never come home last night. I went in to wake him for work a few minutes ago and he wasn't in his bed. You think maybe something bad has happened to him?"

His voice grew smaller and more frightened as he talked, and broke at the end as though he might be going to cry. While I still had his attention, I said, very fast, "Mr. La-Plante, in a few minutes I'm going to send a marked squad car to your house. It'll be white with blue lettering and say 'Rutherford Police Department' on the outside. The officers who come to the door will be in uniform and will show you their identification. They'll take you and Mrs. LaPlante to the building downtown where we'll be transporting the—this person, and you can see for yourself if it's your son. Our officers will stay with you there, and take you home again, and be ready to help you any way they can. Can you do that, Mr. LaPlante, can you and your wife come downtown and help us get this cleared up?" I did my best to make it sound like a community street-cleaning project.

I kept talking till I got him to say yes, but he was coming unstuck fast. I radioed Ed Gray and went over the day duty list with him, looking for a couple of experienced officers to send. We picked Stearns and Donovan. Al Stearns is a couple of years from retirement, he's guaranteed unflappable, and Mary Agnes Donovan has a sweet, soft voice and four boys of her own.

When that was settled, I trotted back to the body, where Pokey was busy with his thermometer and little light.

"Is BCA van coming?" He asked me.

"Yes, but not till later. Probably afternoon. We're gonna have to transport this one ourselves. How about that, Frank, can we ask the fire department for a lift, or—"

"Probably. Yeah, I'll get on it. What about pictures, though? You got your camera with you?"

"Yes. I'll do crime scene, BCA can take the pictures in the lab. We can't keep this body waiting here till afternoon."

"Right on," Pokey said. "I'm gonna get one of lab docs to do autopsy with me, too. No use waiting till tonight or maybe tomorrow for van, huh? Lot better autopsy if we do it now."

Frank got on his radio. I found my camera and went back to the body, where Pokey was sniffing like a hound on a scent. "Funny smell, yah?" he asked me.

"Uh-huh. On the suit, isn't it?"

He leaned toward the blouse and sniffed. "Yah. Smells what, stale?"

"I thought so. And like—old plastic sacks. I noticed it on Wahler, but I was thinking about so many other things at the time that I didn't identify it. Guess it means the suit was stored someplace for quite a while." Frank came back then, and I said, "Smell the suit, Frank." He confirmed the odor, and I asked him, "Whaddaya say about the mask and the chestplate?"

"The mask looks new, or almost. The chest protector looks really old, the old kind of leather straps we were using when I was in school, which is a hundred years ago. That particular glove I happen to know a lot about, because I've bought two of them for Kevin in the last year and a half. Kid can't keep track of spit." Kevin is Frank's fifteen-year-old son. "And the shoes are those same old dogs with metal cleats, like on the Wahler boy." He stared at me pop-eyed again. "Mismatched equipment from several periods, and a suit that's been stored a long time. The killer has access to a storehouse, storeroom, someplace where used equipment is kept. Why not talk to the high schools today, Jake? What have we got, three public and two private? Catholic and Lutheran, that's it for private, isn't it?"

"Right. And Andy Dornoch for the City League stuff."

"Well, sure, although the city doesn't look after—well, he might have a lost-and-found bin. High schools are a better bet. Get somebody in the station to look up the superintendent, principal, whoever's top dog at each school, then call 'em and get 'em to secure the supply rooms right away, and keep the key till you get there, okay? We have got to find out where this equipment is coming from! Oh, shit!" He had spied a van marked "KORN TV" pulling up to the curb. We watched as a reporter and video cameraman piled out.

"Now, how the hell did they get onto this so fast?" Frank fumed. "I'll head 'em off. Here comes the ambulance, get 'em over here quick, will you, Vince? Stay in touch, Jake."

He marched toward the waiting reporter like a good soldier moving toward the sound of the guns. He wasn't going to be facing them alone, though; District Attorney Ed Pearce got out of his car at the curb and hustled directly toward the KORN van, drawn to the TV camera like a moth to the flame. Frank and Ed converged on the crew and began saying as little as possible in very long sentences. The TV reporter, if she thought about it, could probably cut and paste most of what they were telling her out of old crime stories: unfortunate death/no details yet/really can't speculate/more ASAP/keep you fully informed/feel free to call me anytime. Plus, how hard their capable staffs were working.

Frank had learned how to do this part of his job well; he kept the cameraman engaged, so that the lens stayed pointed at him and unable to get past him for a shot of the body. He made eye contact with the reporter, bending his head to her questions as attentively as an anxious suitor. He would say only what he knew for sure: there is a dead person here. Why look like a donkey later because you said too much? But he would find several ways to say it, so she had some quotes to take back with her, and a sound bite to use.

Watching, Pokey shook his head and clucked ironically. "Goodness Gracious, Jake. Frank's really got his bloomers bunched up, huh?"

"Rutherford is his town," I explained, taking pictures as fast as I could point my camera. "He was born here, his folks still live here, and all his brothers and most of their kids. He's been chief six years. He feels responsible for keeping things nice."

"Ah-hah." I might have known Pokey would think that was a hoot. Before he was out of his teens, Adrian Pokornoskovic was repeatedly subjected to social engineering, Soviet style, which he once described to me as, "If bastards ain't froze yet, try starving." The experience left him quick, ironic, and dubious of best-laid plans. He gets a lot of harmless amusement out of the antics of American control freaks.

The guys with the gurney reached us then. I took six more pictures while they set the braces on the legs and unzipped the body bag, and then we hustled off to the lab, roaring past the video cameraman, who took a long fade shot of the outside of the truck. I recognized Greg Prentiss behind the camera. Nice guy, good at his job. The station sends him out to get shots of a crime, he's going to come back with something, even if it has to be tire tracks. I saw him in my rearview mirror focusing on the blood in front of the backstop.

The two local stations rely mostly on network feed to furnish Rutherford news junkies their horror fix around sundown. But while a trailer park wrecked in a tornado in Indiana is always good, and police taking multiple body bags away from a shooting spree in L.A. is very good, local events have the highest impact of all, even when they're smaller. So this one body bag right here in Rutherford, along with the smear of blood in front of the backstop, would get large play on the Rutherford evening news shows. KORN would run the footage of this crime ahead of the pictures of stone-throwing Palestinians, weeping Bosnians, whatever international disasters they brought to our attention tonight. Rutherford folks would give close attention to this calamity, with their beer and peanuts before dinner. Then they would turn the sound down while some senators came on to announce another budget deal, and back up again for the sports and weather.

· S I X ·

STEARNS AND DONOVAN WERE WAITING IN THE CAR WITH the LaPlantes when we drove up to the lab. I realized suddenly that I didn't want the parents in the room when the mask came off. I hustled over to Stearns's side of the car and muttered, "Better wait here a minute. I'll come out and get you, okay?" Stearns just nodded without comment, a brick wall in a blue suit.

I caught up to Pokey at the door and asked, "No reason they have to see the body before we get the genitals out of the mouth, right? We can do that right away, can't we?"

"You betcha. Lessee what they got set up for us here."

We got first cabin service that morning. Somehow, the word was out that we had the possible makings of a serial murder case in Rutherford, and the Hampstead County Pathology Lab wanted a piece of the action. We whizzed right in to the biggest examining room, and the head doc himself, Jason Stuart, was waiting to assist Pokey at the autopsy. I'd seen him once or twice before and privately nicknamed him Dr. Quiet. A small man with sparse gray hair and gray eyes behind rimless glasses, he seldom spoke and almost never smiled. Watching him work was a revelation. He still didn't say much, but his manner became commanding and intense. Work turned him on.

I asked them to leave the uniform on till the parents had been in, so I could find out if they recognized it. Also, remembering our recent wrestling match with Tammy Wahler, I suggested we keep the chopped wrist covered and try to get an identification from just the head. Then, beginning to feel like the stage manager of a horror show, I went out and got the LaPlantes.

They didn't touch or speak, getting out of the car. Coming into the lab, they might have been strangers who had arrived in separate cars. He walked ahead, opening doors for himself, and came to a stop in the middle of the examining room, where he stood silent, gathered into a tight hard knot of dread. She shuffled in after him, shoulders drooping, all her body language insisting, "Feel sorry for me!" She had a hard time getting through the doors we held open for her; she had some resistance to doors. Inside, she shuffled ahead under the blazing lights until she ran up against her husband's back, where she stopped. Her asthmatic wheezing raised the tension in the room several notches; we all watched her, ready to jump if she collapsed.

When Dr. Stuart lifted the sheet off their son's face, they turned toward each other at last, wearing expressions of disbelief, and a sort of puzzlement. I've seen this reaction before. Once, a grieving brother cried out indignantly, "but ... he looks just like always!" People expect some kind of exaltation to take place, a brightness in the expression that says the departed has solved the riddle. But here lay plain old Louie, every inch the barfly and hanger-on, looking scruffy as ever with his potbelly and his three-day stubble. Only now he was silent and cold and dead. Mrs. LaPlante began to make little mewing noises. Her husband moved toward her then, weeping, and put his right arm clumsily over her shoulders, like an awkward suitor trying for his first kiss. He looked across her at me, and asked, "He ain't shot or nothin', is he? What'd he die from?"

"We don't really know that yet, Mr. LaPlante," I said. "These doctors are going to do some tests now to try to find out, and we'll let you know as soon as we know anything." Later, I thought, we'll have to tell them that the body they're getting ready to bury is coming home one hand short. Shoulda seen what the last guy was short of, Mrs. La-Plante. For a minute, I hated my job.

I took them into the foyer. They were overwhelmed, of course, and unable to think clearly. I got very little information from them. Louie had eaten supper at home and then gone out. He didn't say where he was going, he usually didn't.

"Has he ever been married?" I asked, and they both looked up, surprised and slightly shocked, and answered together, "Oh, no ... no," as if family wisdom had decreed, long ago, that Louie was not the marrying kind.

"He worked at the dairy ever since high school," his mother said, as if that explained something.

"I see," I said, and waited, but when she didn't add anything more I asked her husband, "What did he do there?"

"Worked on the bottler, first, on weekends. Then he got on as a handyman helper after he graduated. And he finally worked up to driving a truck, the last coupla years. He liked that, he did pretty well at it, got his own route." He sustained a pleased expression for a few seconds but quickly lapsed into the memory of some long-standing grievance. Squirming and shaking his head, he finally added, "I still had to get him up and see he got to work every morning, though. He stayed just like a little boy that way. His ma looked after his clothes and cooked his meals, all he had to do was get up and go to work, but he never—" He shrugged hopelessly. "Always stayed up half the night is why," he finished. He and his wife exchanged a look, wordlessly continuing some long-standing argument.

They had no idea what he was doing in that ballplayer's uniform; he was certainly not wearing it when he left home last night. He had not played on a softball team since high school. His mother described the clothes he had been wearing when she last saw him—Levi's, a blue T-shirt, a dark green windbreaker. "This ball suit," as she called it, didn't seem quite like the one he had worn in school, either. She was pretty sure she remembered that they had passed his school uniform along to a younger cousin when Louie graduated. Maybe she had a picture of Louie in his ball suit. She would look for it. . . . She was shaken, suddenly, by a storm of coughing.

Stearns shook his head at me then, and Donovan leaned over Mrs. LaPlante and said firmly, "Mrs. LaPlante, why don't you let me help you back to the car, and we'll take you home and you can start to think what you want to do? Is there somebody you'd like to call, to come be with you—?"

The four of them moved together like a badly organized slinky toy, out the door and down the steps. The dreadful whoop of her coughing seemed to echo in the hall for some time after the door closed.

Back inside, Pokey and Dr. Stuart had stripped off the uniform and were weighing and measuring the body. Standing just out of their way, I called the station and was pleased to find Marlys Schultz on the morning support team. Schultzy's a big, bosomy blonde, with five kids and a laugh that rocks the walls. Hidden inside her homey exterior, like a hermit crab in a snail shell, lives an information processor without peer. She's greased lightning on the computer and a walking compendium of databases, but that's just the beginning. She keeps a file as long as your arm of city directories, phone books, professional associations, and club lists, and romps through them as if they were her personal Rolodexes. You want to find a jewelry maker in Denver with relatives still living in Bolivia? A left-handed orthodontist in Cleveland who rides a palomino? Call Schultzy.

Rutherford and its surrounding towns, of course, are just one big backyard to her, almost too easy to be fun. She delivered two names of high school principals just off the top of her head, whipped out their home numbers while I was still writing their names, and had the information on the other three waiting before I had finished talking to the first two.

My timing was just right, too; normal working people were still having breakfast, so I caught every one of the superintendents at home. Frank exerts himself to be helpful to the Rutherford school establishment, and they return the favor. I had confirmation of five storeroom keys in five locked desk drawers, before school started. I checked back with Schultzy; she confirmed that the junior college still doesn't have a softball team, nor do any of the small private Christian schools.

I missed Andy Dornoch at home, and he hadn't arrived at his office yet.

"Keep after him, Marlys, will you?" I asked her. "And when you reach him, tell him I need to talk to him about any softball equipment he might have accumulated in lost-and-found. Ask him when I could see it, will you?"

"I'll find the old buzzard," Schultzy said, "have no fear." She enjoys her reputation as an information guru. "Andy might be a little distracted right now, you know," she added. "His wife's been sick." The downside of Schultzy's itch to know everything is that sometimes she tells you much more than you need. Before she could launch on a description of Mrs. Dornoch's symptoms, I said, "Great work, Schultzy," clicked off, and eased over to the autopsy table to check on progress.

"You see marks on neck?" Pokey lifted a fold of flab and pointed. "Same as before, thin dark line goes all around, harder to see because this guy's fat, but is there if you look for it. Redness and swelling in face, little more pronounced than before. Seems right; this cat wouldn't lose as much blood from end of one arm as Wahler did from that big cut in crotch. Noticeable damage to thyroid cartilage, too, even more than before. Hemorrhages inside eyelids. All evidence of strangulation. Looking very similar, Jake.

"Time of death probably a little later. Rigor mortis just beginning now. Temperature in ear was ninety-two when I got to park. Ninety-one in liver, here in lab, couple minutes ago. Lividity just starting in butt and bottoms of feet. Yah, bottoms of feet again. This body was propped up with feet under, so is natural some blood collected there, but is noticeably more in feet than butt. So. Once again, I'd say your man stood up a while.

"Now *this*—" He turned to the genitals they had taken from the victim's mouth. They were lying on a steel tray on a side table. "Sure wish we coulda tried fitting this back on Wahler, don't you? Too bad he's gone."

"*What?*" I turned on Dr. Stuart. "You let the body go? But I called—"

"This morning." His metallic working voice matched his steel gray gaze, which regarded me coldly behind the twinkly clean glasses. "His wife demanded his release for burial yesterday afternoon. We hadn't received any extraordinary hold orders, and the legal limit without court intervention in Minnesota is three days. We checked with the station to see if they had paperwork that hadn't come over and were told they did not. We did what we had to do."

"Oh, *shit,*" I whispered. "I was counting on a DNA test to prove this penis came from that body. Oh, *goddammit.* I wanted to tie these two cases together so they'd never come apart. It makes so much difference! A serial killer, there's a whole personality profile that goes with that, FBI data banks and who knows what else? Otherwise, maybe all I got here is a copycat. Oh, shit, why didn't they ask me?" I glared helplessly at the body on the table.

"Hey, cool your jets, Honeybunch," Pokey said. "BCA's still got blood from first test, right?"

"Sure, but—"

"That's all they need. Blood in these genitals might be kinda old, but must be some semen left in these testicles, yah?" He looked at Dr. Stuart, who nodded. "Sure. Don't take much for DNA test. Couple drops is plenty. Match with pattern from blood, and there you are. Oughta do plain old blood test first though, maybe save state of Minnesota some money, yah?"

Pokey and Dr. Stuart were nodding to each other like little twin geniuses. Stuart had been almost entirely silent for the first half hour of the autopsy, till he figured out Pokey's freewheeling language skills. Now they were turning into snick and snack, Dr. Quiet and Dr. Noise.

By nine o'clock they were willing to give me a tentative time of death, between midnight and five A.M. I refrained from mentioning that I could have called it that close myself. Blood tests from the penis showed A-positive, same as the Wahler body, they said, so DNA tests were appropriate.

Stuart didn't want to speculate about cause of death until a lot more tests were finished, but Pokey said, "Don't care if tests show mange and epizootic, gonna turn out he got strangled first with thin cord."

I called Schultzy, who told me Andy Dornoch had called his office to say he was doing errands and an interview this morning and would not be in before lunch. She had left my message with his secretary and would stay on his case. I asked her to check with BCA for a time of arrival and to call the social worker at Methodist Hospital to ask when I might see the weeping runner.

"The what?"

"Sorry. Ask her how soon I'll be allowed to interview her

patient, Jerry Creed. The man she picked up at the park this morning."

"Oh, gotcha. Listen, I figured out the fastest route for you to follow to go to all five high schools. You ready?" She made me write it down. I hate taking directions. She's always right about traffic patterns, but in a town this size, what's the difference? Maybe twenty minutes, on the worst day, over the whole trip. It took me half that much time to write down her plan and follow it. If she hadn't gone in for mothering, Schultzy could have had a colorful career as a dominatrix; sometimes I can really see her in leather, with whips.

"Okay, I've got it," I said, "I've *got it*, Schultzy. Gotta go now." Stuart and Pokornoskovic were still deep in gore but assured me they were just finishing up and didn't think they'd have anything significant till the BCA testing was done and the results came back. I drove through brisk morning traffic toward Charles Mangan High School on the east side.

Rutherford's three public schools follow identical policy, I soon learned, for team sports: kids buy their own equipment. If anything's left behind, it's parceled out informally to the neediest kids who sign up the next season. There's always more need than supply, they told me; the lost-and-found bins at each school contained only a few battered scraps.

The two private high schools have similar policies; students buy their own equipment, and any that's forgotten or donated is offered to next year's scholarship students. Their scraps were marginally better and more numerous than the public school leftovers, but neither St. Paul's nor Southern

Minnesota Lutheran boasted the ample supply bins I was looking for. None of the coaches, when questioned, remembered any rash of complaints about missing uniforms or equipment.

All five schools ordered their uniforms plain and had the names put on locally by the alterations staff at one of the department stores. None of their current uniforms quite matched the style and pattern of the suits worn by my two victims. They were all similar, of course, but they had different colored stripes, or wider pants cuffs or longer socks, or a slightly different fabric. In fact it was the fabric that had changed most, I realized; uniform cloth had been getting more and more synthetic and stretchy over the years.

The uniforms on my two victims were distinctly old-fashioned. The principal at Sunnyside High said he thought they had changed styles five or six years ago, and promised to try to find a sample of the old model.

By lunchtime I was sneezing from the dust of many store-rooms and no longer capable of judging whether any of them smelled like the uniform on Frenchy LaPlante. At West Side High, my second-to-last stop, a particularly noxious roach power closed down my sinuses for the rest of the day.

I awarded myself a double cheese baconburger, with fries, to make up for the breakfast I had missed. Food doesn't taste as good when you can't smell it, but I wolfed it down anyway. When I finished I got a take-out coffee and sipped it by my open car door while I called Schultzy.

"I'm kind of stuck in the glue down here, Jake," she said. "Andy Dornoch did call in, at least I got that much for you. He said to tell you he keeps lost-and-found items in a bin behind his office, and he'll see if there's anything in it right now, and if there is you can see it Monday. Said he's busy out of the office all the rest of today.

"But BCA is still swamped in the Twin Cities, can't confirm an ETA yet. And that Erica? At Methodist Hospital? Boy, what a piece of work she is. She says, quote, Jerry Creed has been placed under sedation and is not available, unquote. That's all I could get her to say, Jake."

I put in a call to the hospital. "Erica," I asked her when she answered her page, "is Jerry Creed totally out of it, or what?"

"He's a recovering alcoholic with a history of depression, and the shock of finding a dead body has triggered a great deal of grief and regret. Our Dr. Mason has conferred with his own doctors, and they agree, he's going to have to be monitored carefully for a while. He's been suicidal before, could be again. I expect he'll be available to you as a witness eventually, Mr. Hines, but you'll have to get along without him right now."

I had called her Erica. She was responding by calling me Mr. Hines. Evidently she did not *wish* to be friendly.

"Mr. Creed was the first witness on the scene of a homicide, Ms. North," I said, reading her last name off her card. "What's your best estimate of when he'll be ready to talk?"

"Emotional illness is really impossible to quantify, I'm afraid, Mr. Hines," she said. "He'll be ready when he's ready."

"Well, what's the earliest date I could write down on my calendar, Ms. North, to call and check on his condition? Next Monday? Wednesday? Friday? Help me out here."

There was a little silence, during which I thought I might

have heard her counting backward from ten. Finally she said, "Mr. Hines, it's certainly not my intention to interfere with your investigation in any way. But my first priority, as I explained to you earlier, is to look after the well-being of the patients of this hospital. Now, if you don't feel comfortable with that"—her voice was diamond-hard—"please feel free to call my supervisor, Dr. Mason, and visit with him about your concerns. Do you have his number?" She reeled it off, and I wrote it down, making her repeat it and then listen while I repeated it back to her. I thanked her elaborately for her help and hung up with blood pounding in my ears. I stood staring down at the roof of my car, asking myself, now what the shit was that all about?

It was not really critical that I talk to Creed right away. Cooper had already heard the runner's first impressions of finding the body, and had demonstrated his ability to repeat them almost verbatim. Maddox would fill in the rest. I was just leaning on Erica because, I realized suddenly, the way she used words like "priority" and "comfortable" reminded me of a Family Services functionary named Mrs. Neale, who had governed my life when I was nine. Mrs. Neale took me away from Maxine, the best foster mother I ever had, because she was not comfortable with the fact that Maxine's husband had gotten three to ten at Shakopee for kiting checks.

"Big fucking deal," I said, throwing the f-word in her face in an effort to keep from crying.

"You just proved my point, Jake," Mrs. Neale said. "Now are you ready to accept a more suitable environment, or do you think a little time in Remedial would be more appropriate?" Mrs. Neale knew how to say "appropriate" so it cut like a knife. I'd bet anything Erica liked that word, too.

I tried to think what I had been going to do next after that phone call. Getting mad had wiped out my short-term memory. I gave it up, slid behind the wheel, glanced down at the seat next to me, and found my answer: the pictures I had taken that morning.

We use a young guy named Jay Billingsley for quick developing jobs. He's got a small, struggling studio where he does weddings and graduations while he tries to break into the big time with his stock catalog of nature shots. His contract with us keeps him eating during the lean winter months, and he's still young enough to work double time during the spring-summer rush. He has learned to ignore the content of our pictures and concentrate on making the clearest prints he can out of my unskilled exposures. Usually it's ten incredibly boring shots of a picked lock. The week before last he processed twenty-four pictures of the broken window frame through which those anonymous rascals passed Mrs. Porter's spoons. But sometimes, like now, I have some really bizarre stuff, and I can't just belly up to the bar at Kmart with pictures of a stiff with no hand.

He said he'd get my job out by tomorrow afternoon. I carried on about getting two homicides in one week and how much work I was counting on getting done tomorrow, and finally he said, "Oh, all *right*, Jake, shee, I can't stand to watch a grown man cry. I'll have it for you by seven-thirty tonight."

Leaving his shop, I thought about the interview that I had left over from yesterday. The woman lived alone in a house near Pioneer Park, I remembered. That was on my way back to the station. Maybe I should try to see her now. I wavered: this householder could be imagining things, and I had plenty of work to do. On the other hand, the two cases were beginning to look connected. Eyewitness accounts are worth a ton of printouts, and fresher is always better. I called Schultzy back and asked her to go in my office and read the name and phone number off my calendar.

Anne Condon answered on the second ring. I asked her if this was an okay time to stop by, and she said, "Why, yes, good a time as any," in a dry, no-foolishness voice.

Her address was 844 East Webster, across the street from the park. It's an older residential section in the southeast part of town, a quiet area of modest one-family homes. The Condon house was a two-story stucco bungalow, with a shallow wooden porch set three steps up from its front walk. As soon as the bell chimed inside the house, I heard steady footsteps coming. A gnarled, arthritic hand drew back the lace curtain on the front door. I held my badge up to the glass and a tall, white-haired woman opened the door at once. She was pleasant but businesslike; she got right into her story without a lot of chatting.

She was a light sleeper, she said, and when she woke at night, usually she read for a while till she got sleepy again. "But Monday night was such a nice night, the air smelled so good, I thought I'd just sit by the window a few minutes and enjoy it." She cocked her head. "You want to see where I was sitting?"

"Please," I said.

We climbed narrow wooden stairs to a gently creaking second-floor hall and turned left into the front bedroom. A painted iron bedstead stood against pale wallpaper; her small upholstered chair, with a footstool and a side table, fit comfortably in the bay window.

"Why don't you sit down?" she said. "Then you can see what I was looking at." From Mrs. Condon's chair, I looked through her window at the side gate of Pioneer Park, directly across the street.

"I had just decided to turn on the lamp and find my book, but then this big truck drove up and stopped by the park, and a man got out and started unloading a shipment, so I thought I'd just watch a while. You don't expect a park to get deliveries in the middle of the night. But they did, that night. The driver opened the doors in back and climbed in and wheeled something onto the back platform and lowered the platform, you know how they do? With some kind of a hydraulic hoist? The step drops partway to the ground. Then he slid the metal glides of the two-wheeler along the edge of the step, you know, to lower it the rest of the way, and wheeled it over to the gate, and on through."

"Oh through? Didn't he have to unlock the padlock first?"

"Well, yes, sure. He had to pull it out from the other side of the gate, of course, because they lock up those padlocks from the inside at night. I've watched them doing it. I've lived here for thirty years almost, I know the routine at this park pretty well. He pulled the padlock out and unlocked it, wheeled his carrier inside, and pulled the padlock back inside and locked it again."

"Locked it?" I said. "You're sure?"

"Yes, you can see that from up here I can see over the top of the gate, and I saw his hands come up and push the prongs of the padlock through the wire loop. Then he went off there in the dark and delivered whatever it was he had stacked on that two-wheeler, and came back out and put the two-wheeler in his truck and drove away."

"Did he lock the gate?"

"Well no, that's what was so curious, that's why I remembered it. I told those other police officers who were here, didn't they tell you?"

"They just left me a note," I said. "You mind telling me again?"

"Well, I mean, that's the whole point of the story, that's why I remembered it when they came asking if we saw anything unusual here in the neighborhood. It seemed so odd that he would lock up after himself when he went in, and then leave the gate open when he came out."

"He left it standing open? Not just unlocked but open?"

"That's right. I thought about calling 911 to report it, but then it seemed like such a small thing, and I didn't know, maybe he left it open for somebody else who was coming right behind him, you know? And then I'd just be causing a lot of trouble for nothing. So I turned on my light and read for a few minutes, and then went back to sleep. But the gate was still open when I went back to bed."

"What time was that?"

"About a quarter past one."

"And it had been open about, what, half an hour by then?"

"Something like that. Let's see, it was just about midnight when I woke up. I sat there a few minutes before the truck drove up. The delivery man was probably inside for about fifteen minutes. Or twenty? So he was out again and gone before one o'clock. And the gate was standing open from then on."

"And later on that night, when we found the body and all the police cars came, did you hear any of that?"

"Not a thing! Isn't that funny? But that's how it is with me these days, more and more as I get older. I wake up and go to sleep on my own schedule, and what's going on around me doesn't make that much difference."

"Okay. One other thing—you mentioned a stack. Did you see something like that, a stack of boxes, or—?"

"Well, I guess I said that because that's what you do carry on one of those things, isn't it? My husband and I used to run a little grocery store, maybe you remember it, Condon's Groceries, down on North Broadway?"

"Oh, sure, that building has been remodeled now, hasn't it? Let's see, what went in there?"

"Tastee Freez. We sold to them. Anyway I've stacked my share of boxes on a two-wheeler. But actually I couldn't see what was on this one, because he had a cover, like a tarp, wrapped around it and held on with canvas straps."

"Oh, is that right? So it could have been just one item, you mean, and not a stack of boxes?"

"Could have been anything, that's right. It was one of the big two-wheelers, like they use to move washers and big pieces of furniture. As tall as the man who was pushing it. And whatever he had on it was as tall as the cart."

"And you're sure it was a man? Doing the delivery?"

"Pretty sure. Walked like a man, wore a man's heavy work shoes and leather gloves and a man's canvas hat, like a fishing hat, with the brim turned down all around."

"What about the truck? Any name on the truck?"

"Uh . . . well. I feel bad about that. There probably was a name on the door, but I didn't look for it particularly, and in the dark . . . I just didn't see if there was a name on it. But it was a big cargo van, Dodge or Chevy, diesel I think from the sound of it, with mud guards on the back wheels."

"Mrs. Condon," I said, "I wish I could put you on steady." She laughed delightedly, sounding suddenly young, and said, "Well, that's a deal, I'll do the snooping and you can nab the bad guys, okay?" We shook hands, and I left my card in case she thought of anything else.

I called Andy Dornoch's office. His secretary said, "He's checking picnic tables at the new campground out by the fairgrounds. He said he'd call you about the lost-and-found stuff, didn't you get the message?"

"Yep," I said, "but I need the answer to another question, now. Will you ask him to let me know what delivery normally gets made to Pioneer Park after midnight Monday night?"

She made me repeat the second half of the message, and then read it back to me incredulously, "—*after midnight Monday night?*" Finally she said, "Oookay, I'll put it on his desk," making it clear she was humoring me.

·SEVEN·

THE SWING SHIFT WAS GETTING BRIEFED IN THE SQUAD room when I got back to the station. The seven-to-three crews, going off, were changing clothes and chattering around the coffeepot in the break room, trying to cool out so they'd be fit to face kids and shopping and housework. One of the hardest things about being a cop is learning to stop being a cop when your shift is over. Some days you never quite make it.

I went in to fill my coffee mug and collided with Miller.

"Hey, Jake. You notice how my new pup can drive? Pretty good, huh?"

A pup is a trainee, at least in Rutherford; he was talking about Amy Nguyen. "I saw," I said. "Looked like you were getting along real well."

"She pays attention," he said defensively. "I don't have to tell her twice. I like that."

"How's it going with the Glock? She still scared to shoot?"

"She never was scared. That's not the problem. I got Wiggy to figure it out."

"You turned Wiggy loose on her?" I asked him. "Already? Jeez, Les. Now she'll quit for sure."

John Wiggerstaff is Rutherford's law enforcement firearms instructor, a demure-looking former altar boy who, on the firing range, unexpectedly turns into a scary tyrant. An uncompromising perfectionist with a talent for quiet contempt, he has reduced many a macho hero to humility. We all have to get our shooting technique rechecked by Wiggy a couple of times a year. It's about as much fun as a broken arch. During my last review, he looked at me coldly through his round wire-rims and asked, "You want to get shot, is that it?" I sincerely do not want to get shot; otherwise, I would never put up with Wiggy.

"John's hard on the older hands, because he worries that we'll get complacent and have an accident," Les said. "With new recruits, he's as patient as can be. He watched Amy shoot a couple of rounds and pinpointed her problem right away. I didn't see it, because it never happened to me. But you know how the Glock ejects a shell out the top, sort of throws it over your shoulder? Well, to make that work right, the forearm and wrist need to be rigid, so the recoil will throw the shell casing up and out. Amy only weighs a little over a hundred pounds, so she's having trouble handling the kick. Her first shot is likely to go high, and then the shell tends to stovepipe because her hand and wrist are too soft. Stovepipe, you know? Gets a funny torque on it, starts to sort of waddle instead of coming straight up and out, next thing you know it hangs up in the ejection cylinder. Then she's got a jammed gun and can't fire a second round."

Les Miller sipped his coffee and beamed at me. "But! I've got so many resources now that I didn't have just a few years ago! Once Wiggy analyzed the problem, we called our sports medicine guy at the clinic. He prescribed exercises on those machines at the gym. We're gonna give her power forearms." He chuckled at the prospect of turning his tiny trainee into Ms. Popeye.

"You think you can get her up to strength soon enough, so the guys won't bitch about riding with her?"

"Oh, sure. Amy's an athlete, she'll get there fast. She's a marathon runner, Jake, you know how long those damn marathons are?" Where have I heard this song before? "And she fits right in with the crews, the guys are already calling her Winnie." He went humming off to his charts. FTOs get a big stake in their pups, whose success rate validates their training methods. Last year, Les Miller boasted for weeks about a handsome, athletic trainee of his who was going to make us all pull up our socks. He turned out to be a dyslexic near-illiterate, whose admiring mother, sisters, and coaches had been helping him fake reading and writing all through school. Les nearly went up a wall when it turned out his bright star couldn't handle routine paperwork.

Hearing my phone ring, I ran for my office. Marlys Schultz said, "Mrs. Porter's on the phone. You got anything new on her stuff, Jake?"

"No, oh, jeez," I said, feeling my soul shrivel. "Schultzy, could you possibly—?"

"Sure. I figured you had enough to do, that's why I asked. Jake"—her voice dropped—"does it look like we've got some kinda maniac loose in our little village?"

Schultzy isn't looking for kicks, and she has no time for gossip. But she watches over a big nest; besides five kids, she and her husband both have elderly parents beginning to need help.

"I can't say for sure, Marlys," I told her, "but two bad things have happened in four days, and they're a lot alike. So, yeah, it's time to sit everybody down and explain about using their brains and staying close."

"Thanks, buddy." She sucked air. "I'll tell Mrs. Porter we're thinking of putting the dogs on her punch bowl."

I went looking for Frank. His door was open, but his chair was empty; in his outer office Lulu Breske, wearing a headset over her yellow corkscrew curls, was rapidly filling the blanks on a phone-message pad while keeping a word processor humming. I tore a sheet of paper out of my spiral notebook and wrote, "I think I know how the first body got to the park," signed it, and folded it twice.

I asked Lulu, "Will you give this to Frank?" She tore a pink Post-it note off a little pad, stuck it in a date-and-time stamper, wrote on it, "Per: Jake," slapped it onto my note, and tossed the whole thing into Frank's in basket. Comes the Apocalypse, I look for Lulu to slap a timed, dated pink Post-it note on it, with a notation, "Per: God."

Back in my office, I called the records desk in St. Paul, asked for Tom Eckert, the talented searcher I'd been talking to all week, and described the many similarities between the first and second killings. His reaction was swift and emphatic.

"If you think you might be looking for a serial killer, Jake," he said, "that's a federal file. A much more limited, restricted-use file. I didn't search it before, because serial killers are in a class by themselves. And I have to request access from the FBI. I'll get on it right away."

"How fast can you get in?" I asked him. "When can I see the results?"

"I'll stay tonight till I finish it," he said, "and fax you everything I find. No, no, it's no trouble. To be honest, I'm looking forward to it. I don't get to work with this file very often. I'll just get my girlfriend to hold dinner. Boy, though," he said, in a burst of candor that raised the hair on the back of my neck, "I hope you don't have a serial killer. Those guys are *weird*."

He regretted his lapse immediately, scuttling back onto safe bureaucratic turf. "I'll call your desk when I get this put together," he said, "and get them to keep the line free for the fax, and I'll watch to be sure it goes through. You should have my results by late evening." His voice trailed off vaguely, and I could tell I no longer had his full attention. He was already plotting the search.

I was typing up notes an hour later when my phone rang. It was Jimmy Chang.

"Jake," he said, "have I got this right? You got a serial killer down there?"

"You said that, pal," I told him. "I don't even have a cause of death for my second victim yet, for sure. You coming down here pretty soon?"

"I'm trying to fix it so I do," he said. "They had me assigned to a couple of other things tonight, but as soon as I heard what you've got in Rutherford I got hot on the phone with the powers that be. I've urged them to consider that with a serial killer at large they'll be wasting time and resources if they don't send the same crew that did the first one." He chuckled. "You realize what you got down there, ol' buddy? My Ph.D. thesis is what you got! Shee, a break like this comes along so rarely! Serial killers, everybody talks about them, but in fact I know guys that've been doing forensic work for *years* and never had one! So yes indeed, absolutely, I hope to see you in a couple hours."

"Sure glad you're pleased, Jimmy," I said. "Just don't forget about my DNA tests, huh?"

"For sure," he said. "I'm gonna be very careful about matching up hair and fibers on those two uniforms, too, Jake. Be sure they keep that second uniform away from any contamination till I get it! And dirt on the shoes could be important, too. Every little thing will count when it comes to hanging these two cases together. This is the big one I've been waiting for, don't let anybody screw it up!"

"Tell you what, Jimmy," I said, "On the next one, we'll try to get you in on the killing, that way you can supervise it right from the beginning and be sure nothing goes wrong."

There was a frozen silence, and then he said softly, "Was this guy a friend of yours, Jake?"

"Nah," I said, "it looks a little different from down here, is all. Sorry."

"Well," he said, "if I was being insensitive, I apologize. I didn't mean—"

"Forget it," I said. "Call me when you're ready to leave St. Paul, will you?"

I called Dr. Stuart to make sure we had the lab time

saved. He indicated a keen desire to assist in Chang's tests. Everybody wanted a piece of Louie now. I told him I'd see to it.

Pokey was between patients when I called. He came to the phone saying, "So, those twinkies from Twin Cities finally gonna stir their stumps, hah?"

"Uh-huh. But they still didn't have a van ready last I heard, so I'll call you as soon as I hear anything. You be home?"

"Friday night, you kiddin'?" Pokey snorted. "I'll be at topless bar gettin' down like always." I know he's married, and I've never seen him in a bar, so I suppose that was a joke. Sometimes it's hard to tell. He said, "Call me as soon as you know, hah?" and hung up in my ear.

I got down a fresh red loose-leaf binder, labeled it "LaPlante," and set it up the same as the Wahler file, a chronological statement of events, followed by tagged separators for the test results and pictures that would start going in it tomorrow. I put the two of them side by side on the shelf above my desk, with stacks of software manuals for bookends.

"Now, damn, it," I said softly to no one in particular, "that's all the colors I've got on hand, so let's cut out the shit, okay?" I asked the desk to watch out for Tom's fax and to page me when Jimmy Chang called. Then I walked quietly out of my office and out of the building. It would be an exaggeration to say that I tiptoed; I deny tiptoeing. Admittedly, I did hear Frank, at the far end of the hall, ask somebody, "Jake in his office?" just as I started down the back stairs. But I had been working for almost twelve hours, and I was hungry and thirsty. I had a full evening at the lab still ahead, and I wanted a few minutes alone. So yeah, if you insist, I kind of snuck out of the building.

I went to a little restaurant named Sons, a tall, carpeted room with many pictures on one side and a small loft on the other. It's owned by three friends of mine, named Peterson, Anderson, and Gustafson.

"I see it as a homey, comfortable place, but distinctly upscale," Per Gustafson told me when they were getting ready to open. Per is the entrepreneurial type who finds the money and handles promotion. "We're going to do classic prairie food with just a touch of nouvelle cuisine."

"What does that mean, exactly?" I asked.

"It means we won't call it mousse if it's pudding," Gus Anderson said, "but we won't feed you canned peas, either." He's the chef. He looks like a blond gorilla. He's a great kidder till he starts to cook; then he grows fangs and claws.

Scott Peterson usually takes the door. He's got a nice light touch with customers and a firm, steady one for the staff. The Sons have been open about a year and a half, and I get the impression they've quit having nightmares about bankruptcy court.

I was so early, I had my pick of tables. I got Scott to put me upstairs under a light. He brought me a half-liter of chardonnay and the evening paper. A tall headline screamed, "Mutilation Slayer Strikes Again."

There was a picture of a younger Louie LaPlante, smiling in a suit and tie. A second photo, taken today, showed his parents sitting side by side on a couch, holding the same portrait between them. They looked embarrassed as hell, which seemed reasonable to me. The story had most of the basic details correct, but still omitted mention of the Polaroid pinned to the uniform. Frank was convinced that the picture was somehow the key to the puzzle, and he was determined to keep it a closely held secret.

Looking up, I met the cool, quizzical stare of my host.

"Late dinner trade might be a little light for a while," I admitted. "We're working on it, Scott. Believe me."

"I never doubted it," he said, ever the diplomat. "Anything else I can bring you?"

"You got anything else around to read?"

He brought me an old copy of *Popular Science*. I sat sipping cold wine in the pretty, quiet room, reading a story about a recently discovered way to extract energy from the stored heat in the sea. Hurray, technology's going to save us all. Then I turned a few more pages and found an appalling list of things society is doing to mess up the world's oceans. Boo, hiss, technology's killing us as we speak.

When my walleye arrived, I put the magazine under my chair to concentrate on perfectly broiled fish and crisp hot vegetable spears. I was almost finished when my beeper sounded. Jimmy Chang said he had his assignment and his van and was on his way.

"I got the same photographer again, too, Trudy Hanson. We're going to do a bang-up job for you, Jake."

I told him we'd all be waiting for him. Jimmy was being extra cordial, anxious to mend fences after my show of temper. And I found it easy to return his friendliness after he told me he'd be bringing Trudy Hanson along.

I called Pokey and the lab and then called Frank at home. He came to the phone from outside somewhere, saying, "Thought I lost you."

"I'm headed back to the lab, BCA finally freed up a van."

"You think maybe I better come down?"

"Nah. For what? Any decisions to make, I'll call you. Otherwise, you know how it is, mostly gobbledegook we can't understand anyway, till they translate it into English. What I wondered, Frank, you got a couple hours in the morning? I know it's Saturday, but I thought if we could have a little time together, I'd like to lay out a couple of things, see what you think."

"Fine," he said. "Can we make it early? I promised to um- pire an Elks Lodge tournament at nine."

"Seven too early? Gonna take a little time."

"Seven's fine." He meant it. The last time Frank slept in was probably during the Kennedy administration. "Jake? You talked to the FBI yet?"

"Not exactly. BCA is searching their records for me. It's one of the things we have to decide about, calling in the FBI. If this really is a serial killer, we'll want all the help we can get, right?"

"Sure. And I like to initiate the action from here, you know. Not have them call us." St. Paul sent the Feds down to take over a kidnapping case from Frank, a couple of years ago. They were pretty condescending. I guess it still smarts.

"I know. Let's decide in the morning." I paid my tab and drove out to Twenty-fourth Street, where Jay was watching for me through the sidelight by his front door; he'd been closed for ten minutes. He turned the key in the lock, handed out my pictures without a word, and locked up again immediately. I glanced at the prints at curb side just enough to ensure they were adequate. I wanted to save first impressions till I was in my office in good light.

I was still a little early, so I decided on a fresh-air fix. I parked three blocks from the lab and strolled the rest of the way through the fragrant late-May dusk. Fat was sizzling on a backyard barbecue somewhere, a dog barked aimlessly, two cars full of adolescents paused in an intersection to yell at each other and then speed away, leaving rubber. Five preteen boys on Rollerblades blithely defied death on the parking ramp behind Security Bank. A pair of lovers nuzzled along the sidewalk past Methodist Hospital, oblivious to everything but passion. Spring had turned all our tickers up.

The lab parking lot was empty when I walked into it; I stood by the door a couple of minutes, till Pokey pulled in and parked.

"Need to ask you something," I said, when he walked up to me.

"Oh?" He got three syllables into it, expressing everything from, "I should hope so," to "This should be a pip."

"This morning at the park? When I showed you what was behind the mask? I got the impression maybe you'd seen that before."

"Ah, yah." He sighed. "Plenty times. Sorry to say. That stuff happening in Bosnia last year, on TV every night, everybody yelling outrage, outrage? Is nothing new, Jake." His foxy little face, half-lit by the glow from the streetlamp, looked rueful and weary. He shrugged and twisted his neck around, like somebody trying to get out of a yoke. "Never expected to see it here, though. In this nice, peaceful town—" He shook his head. "Very surprising." He stared off into the lilacs at the edge of the parking lot for a couple of minutes, his lips working. Then he added, "Is usually where there's war, you know? Two sides, or three or four, they get plenty of hate going. People get convinced they got grievance, other side is evil, then they violate their dead that way."

"Okay," I said, leaning toward him, hurrying now because I saw the BCA van pulling in. "But what does it *say*, Pokey? What's the message?"

"Message?" He stared at me a minute, then nodded approvingly. "Ah. Well. Lotta times, you're right, Jake, genital mutilation is response to rape. Like maybe, one side overruns a place, rapes a bunch of the women, other side takes town back or captures some of the troops, they'll cut off their cocks and stick 'em down their throats like that. To say, 'Here, you so proud of this pecker, chew on it awhile.' Is biggest possible injury to give back for worst possible insult, yah?"

"Uh-huh. So you're saying—revenge."

"Well, yah, revenge or . . . hate, anyway, to say dirty dog, you lower than a pig . . . People don't do terrible things like that just for fun of it. Or not where I come from, anyway." He made a sound somewhere between a snort and a laugh. "Who knows why American would do it? Is big strange country, lotsa possibilities I guess." We watched the BCA crew beginning to unload their baskets of goodies. Pokey sighed again, more cheerfully this time.

"Is sure cute, that long yellow braid, huh?" he mused. Trudy looked up and waved at us, and Pokey hustled over, saying, "My goodness, Trudy, so many pieces! Here, let me help you with that. Here, come on, Jake, help Trudy carry all this heavy stuff."

"Glad to see you," I said, and dropped one of her bags. Old Jake, all smooth moves and original lines.

She began handing me zippered nylon camera bags, saying, "Oh, aren't you nice! Oh, are you sure you can carry one more?" as if I was King Kong clambering up the Empire State Building on her behalf. She was wearing a pink sweater that fit really well.

Jimmy protested, from behind his own mountain of equipment, "Jeez, guys, what is this, sex discrimination?" and Pokey assured him, "Damn betcha, better believe it." Then, relenting, he handed me a couple more of Trudy's bags and picked up some of Jimmy's stuff. We all staggered toward the glass doors, which, suddenly illuminated as we moved toward them, revealed Dr. Stuart with his hand on the switch, with two immaculate white-coated assistants beside him in the shining hall.

Jimmy threw a fit when he learned that the two local doctors had gone ahead with an autopsy on the brain and internal organs without him.

"This will compromise all my findings!" he wailed. "I'll be dealing with secondhand information!"

Dr. Stuart stared him down. "All our findings are fully documented, signed off by Dr. Pokornoskovic and me, as well as one or more of my assistants. And they're certainly more valid than if we'd waited till you got here, Mr. Chang." All glinty and gray behind his squeaky-clean glasses, he put a tiny emphasis on the word "mister" that made Trudy Hanson look up from her camera, then go back to shooting pictures wearing a tiny smile.

Pokey was helping her take pictures of the victim's neck.

He wanted to be sure she showed the thin line left by the garrotte, but it was difficult because of the fat rolls. Once they agreed they'd done the best they could with the outside of the neck, they spent a long time positioning lights to show the broken hyoid bone.

Jimmy began taking blood and tissue samples, looking aggrieved. Then Stuart told him about the Wahler body being gone, and the need to get DNA material from what was probably a four-day-old penis. The two of them became absorbed in arcanum about molecular decomposition. I couldn't follow where their whirlwind of Latin and initials led them, but it was fun to watch the pursuit of truth melting the frost off their relationship.

Trudy finished fingerprinting and got ready to haul all her gear back outside.

"Let me help you," I said. "You really ought to have a little burro that you bring along in the back of that van."

She giggled. "Jimmy and I have been thinking about a robot," she said. "Sort of R2D2 with maybe eight arms."

"One could be a snow shovel," I suggested.

"Well, right, and one a clothespin, for evidence bags," she said, "and there could be one with ten fingers to hold both our coffee cups, we thought." Back inside, she began asking Jimmy, "These ready to go? How about this?" And we made another trip to the parking lot, enlarging the task list for the robot as we worked. Trudy wanted to free up two hands for fingerprinting, and I suggested we make one arm end in a hand with a telephone receiver, and program his chip to handle routine calls. He could cluck sympathetically to people whose stolen items had not been found, and assure anxious callers that a capable staff was working on the crime and we would keep the public fully informed. I did a demo call between R2D2 and Millicent Porter. By the time we had the van loaded, we were having quite a jolly time. We got back inside the lab just as the doctors were getting ready to put the body away.

"So now," I said quickly, "shouldn't we all go someplace for coffee, before we send this poor girl back out on the road to drive all the way to St. Paul in the dark?"

Jimmy Chang started looking at his watch, his prim little overachiever's mouth open to protest that there was no time for that. But Pokey stifled his disapproval, throwing a convivial arm over Jimmy's slender shoulders and shouting, "Damn tootin'! All finished with blood and guts, time for dessert, yah?" He herded everybody out to the parking lot, loaded Chang into his car, got Stuart to agree to follow him, and told me to meet him at Charlie's. I helped Trudy tenderly into my car, a somewhat ludicrous gesture to make toward a paid-up member of the Teamster's Union, but it felt good. She was too good a driver for me to try any funny detours, but I made the two blocks to the restaurant as slow as I could.

It was past eleven o'clock, and we were all on the edge of exhaustion, I guess, so that as soon as we sat down and relaxed, we began to get giddy over trifles. Jimmy said he just wanted a cup of tea, but when Pokey insisted he should keep his strength up, he went apeshit and ordered Black Forest cake à la mode. After that we all competed to try to find the most sumptuous desserts on the menu, piling one wretched excess on top of another. I got a sundae so large it came in a soup bowl, with five different sauces and chopped nuts. Even Jason Stuart unbent; he asked for decaffeinated coffee with his cheesecake and then said, "Oh, hell, gimme the real stuff," and we gave him a deafening round of applause.

When we had reached satiety and were dipping our napkins in our water glasses to sluice off some of the sticky places, Pokey asked idly into a sudden silence, "The baseball games these local guys play, they pretty good? Like paid guys on TV?"

"Well—if you're asking about the guys we've been talking to this week, Pokey," I said, "they don't play baseball. They play softball."

"Aah. Is much different?"

"Sure. They use a bigger ball, a little softer than a baseball, and a smaller field. And the pitcher throws underhand."

"Used to be a damn good game, though," Dr. Stuart said, "when it was fast-pitch. But all that changed in the late sixties, early seventies, when the new rules came in. Slow-pitch softball is for wusses," he said firmly.

"Oh, well, now," Jimmy said, "I don't know about that. I belonged to a slow-pitch league in Minneapolis for a couple of years, and we had some darn good players."

"Three balls, two strikes, quit after the seventh inning if the time's up? *Pitiful*," Stuart said, his face a mask of contempt. It was fun watching him get excited. "They just changed everything to make it easier for the women's teams, if you ask me."

"Oh, sure," Trudy said, "now we're going to blame it on the women."

"Don't take no insults, sweetheart," Pokey said, "give him who-for."

"You mean what-for," I said.

"He does?" Jimmy asked. "How can you be sure?" Was the moon full? Jimmy Chang had made a joke!

"Now fast pitch," Stuart said, undeterred, "we used to have some really hairy contents, Pokey. Wish you could have seen the game in those days. An underhand pitcher can throw a ball so fast you can't see it, sometimes. And when somebody really connects with a bat to a ball going a hundred miles an hour, Holy Moses, that baby will *travel*."

"What position did you play?" I asked him. I was really interested; it was hard to imagine this tightly wrapped guy ever playing anything. Besides, I wanted to keep him talking. I was sitting next to Trudy in the crowded booth; she had wonderful soft places, and smelled good.

"Second base, usually. Or shortstop. I liked second base best because you get to do two jobs really, you know, cover the base and the infield both. Plenty of action. I made two outs of a triple play, once," he announced, smiling dreamily at the memory.

"Really? I've always dreamed of being in on a triple play," I said. "Runners on what, first and second?"

"Yup. The batter hit a line drive right to me. Really burned it in, damn near knocked me down. But I caught it, so that put the hitter out, of course. Then, well, runners can't lead off, you know, in softball the way they can in baseball," he explained to Pokey, who was already beginning to look like a man who'd heard more than he ever needed to know about this subject. "But they can start to run as soon as the pitcher throws the ball, and of course both of those guys did, that day. I tagged the second-base runner before he could get back. Actually," he said, staring into the middle distance, galvanized by a memory that must be over thirty years old, "I coulda had the whole thing unassisted, if I'd been sure.... The first-base runner had run a little too far. By the time he got himself turned around and headed back to first, I had the other runner out, and I could have caught him, I was fast in those days. But the coach and everybody on the team started yelling, 'Throw it, throw it!' so I did, and the first baseman got credit for the third out." He shook his head mournfully.

"Even so, you must have felt terrific," Jimmy said. "Did you win the game?"

"Huh?" It took Dr. Stuart a few seconds to get back to us. "I don't know. I don't remember anything else about that game, just that one play."

"You ever play on a team?" I asked Trudy. I didn't care what she answered. I just wanted to keep on sitting the way we were.

She shook her head vigorously. "I don't like team sports. I like to go at my own pace, skiing, swimming, that kind of stuff."

That gave Jimmy Chang the chance he'd been waiting for, to look at his watch and say, "Listen, we better go at our own pace back to St. Paul before it gets any later, huh?" Something ought to be done about Jimmy Chang's unremitting work ethic, I decided. The poor lad was headed for burnout, and taking this delightful young woman with him. We all started pushing chairs back and groping for the check, till Pokey announced he had already paid it.

"Decided I better show some appreciation," he said

grandly, "getting all this extra business from department, and then lessons about baseball free gratis on top."

"Softball, Pokey, jeez, pay attention, willya? *Softball*," I said. But he wasn't listening. He was winking at Trudy, who rewarded him with a conspiratorial giggle that made his wrinkles blush.

·EIGHT·

SATURDAY MORNING'S BLAZING DAWN LOOKED LIKE THE backdrop for a tourism brochure featuring happy, whiskery guys in fishing boats. I thought longingly about the river as I drove downtown, and took another long, wistful sniff of lilac-scented morning before I went inside. Once I reached the seasonless, fluorescent-lighted dead air of the second floor, though, distractions faded and the job started cranking me up. I made a fresh pot of coffee, filled my mug to the brim, and began organizing the material I wanted to show Frank.

Rutherford PD occupies the whole second floor of the Municipal Building. The office space downstairs is split between the city and county, and when they're closed, on weekends and holidays, RPD has the building to itself. So one compensation for working on Saturday is the quiet, private feel my office has on those days. With the closed door between me and the hustle at the duty desk, and not a peep coming up from the tax assessor's office below, Saturday morning is Concentration City.

I spread my LaPlante pictures out, turned on all the lights in the room, and stared at them for ten minutes. In a couple of the shots, I convinced myself I could see a couple of fragmented wheel prints in the sand near the body; I put those prints on top, to show Frank. I was rearranging the Wahler prints when Frank stuck his head in, said, "Let's use my office," and went on down the hall.

Oh, hell! It was only twenty minutes to seven! Why was he here so early? I felt like one of the three little pigs: can't get ahead of that damn wolf. I wanted a few more minutes to consider the FBI option and ponder my growing list of riddles. But I could feel him in there, drumming on his desk, staring at the door, and I didn't want him to start off impatient. I took down my three-ring binders, stacked the pictures and printout and steno pad on top, and muscled the armload out the door.

The hall was filled with the clamor of night duty squads checking out. Vince Greeley fell into step with me, saying, "Hey, Jake! Whaddaya think of this crazy week? Aside from the crazy hours and the crazy phone calls and the crazy killers, it's not a bad week, huh?"

"Hey, no sweat," I said, "I'm gonna have enough vacation time piled up to go to Papua New Guinea for a month."

"Pa-who-a New–what's-a? You better get a new travel agent, pal, you're way out of the mainstream. Boy," he jabbered along down the hall with me, gregarious as most cops are at the end of a night shift, glad to leave the lonely dark behind, "people are really up in arms about these killings, aren't they? My neighbors are all *over* me, you'd think I whacked these guys myself personally. They keep grabbing me every time I go out to get in my car, saying, 'What about this, Vince, we gonna be safe in our beds here or what?' I told my wife, I think I better figure out some way to go to the grocery store in-cog-*nee*-toe."

"Uh-huh. Vince? Question I've been wanting to ask you. You ever see Wahler and LaPlante together? Were they friends, that you know of?"

"Not that I knew," Greeley said. "Best I can remember, Jake, I never laid eyes on James Wahler till I found him dead. But Frenchy LaPlante, you could just about count on him being at most of the Rutherford games, and around the players' hangouts after. He kind of hero-worshiped athletes, liked to be around 'em and talk to 'em."

"But there was no connection between the two men that you know of, till they turned up dead in the same uniform?"

"Guess it *is* the same uniform, isn't it? What team's it belong to, by the way?"

"I still don't know. Doesn't quite match any of the schools. None of the City League players that I've talked to have identified it. And there's no name on it, so—"

Vince laughed and punched my shoulder. "Life's a bitch and then you die, right? Hang in there, buddy." He headed for the lockers.

"Could I ask Harley, you think? He still around?" I called after him. Vince turned at the door of the locker room and said, "Mundt took a personal day last night. He's got this weekend off, and he's helping his brother build a garage. I worked with Bailey last night." He crossed his eyes and pan-

tomimed shooting himself in the ear. "I been listening to
no-good-wife complaints for *eight hours*." I laughed and
hurried on down the hall.

The chief was leaning against his desk with his arms
folded, wearing his kill-the-British expression. "You get
your call from the paper yet?" he asked before I was all the
way into the room.

"The paper?" I said, getting that feeling you get right after you've hit a deer in the dark, that feeling that says, "Oh
shit, trouble," even before you bump your nose on the
windshield.

"Somebody from this department phoned in an anonymous tip about those goddamn pictures. Jim Burgess called
me at home last night, said they'd received this phone call
from somebody who wouldn't give his name but gave very
detailed information about the pictures that were on the
bodies. Jim was able to describe 'em to me to *perfection*. He
said of course they'd never print anything on an anonymous phone call, but he thought it was kind of sneaky of
me to hold something back like that without letting him
know I was doing it.

"Shit!" Frank punished the rug with his huge, heavy
shoes. "You know how hard I've worked to get good rap-
port with the media." He pronounced it "re-pour." "I told
him we thought it was important to have a few details un-
published, something we might be able to use to evaluate a
suspect when we got one. But Burgess said, look, this is an
independent source, I don't feel I can sit on this and do
nothing, if you don't help me I'm going to have to start
nosing around. In the end, what I had to do, I brought 'em

both down here, Burgess and Task together so I wouldn't get accused of favoring print over TV, and *showed* them the goddamn pictures, so they could see they would never want to print them in a family newspaper or show them on the local station. They took notes, you shoulda seen *that*. They're going to think of some acceptable way to describe them, they say, starting tonight. Can you beat that?" Frank said, flouncing around his office like an outsize mother hen that just got chased off her nest. "Some *acceptable* way to describe them! How the bloody Christ do you suppose they'll do that? A body with its pecker carved off, and another guy with the damn thing shoved down his throat?"

"Did he say if it was a male or a female?" I asked. "The caller?" I thought maybe a simple question or two might cool him down. I should have known.

"I asked him. He didn't want to say. *They* have to protect their *sources*." He did a devastating imitation of the editor's prim little lisp. "What the Christ do I get to protect? If I find out who made that call," Frank promised, "I am going to have his head on a pike by the front gate! Sonofabitch! Didn't I fully explain my purpose, wasn't I explicit with you?"

"Yes," I said.

"Well, then! Who'd you forget to tell?"

"Nobody," I said, as firmly as if I was sure. And I was, almost. I had done the best I could to pass the word to everybody, all along the trail of people who had anything to do with those pictures, that the chief insisted they remain a secret. But even if I hadn't, why would anybody from the department phone the paper? Any cop I've ever known would rather squirt seltzer up his nose than get a reporter on his tail.

"Bullshit!" Frank roared. "Somebody dropped the dime, and I wanna know who it was! This is important! You're gonna make me up a list of everybody who handled those pictures, and we're gonna have a Come to Jesus meeting and get to the bottom of this!"

"Fine," I said, beginning to get really pissed myself. I was buried in work already; I didn't need any list-making chores. Besides, I'd rather fight alligators in a slime pit than attend one of Frank's Come to Jesus meetings. I mean, grown men sitting around in blue uniforms with tears in their eyes? Give me a break.

"Let's all sit down and make little lists," I hollered at him. "Why don't we start a whispering campaign too? That way you can get everybody in the department mad at everybody else! Then this freaky killer that we came down here to talk about can keep right on having fun, chopping up guys in parks. We won't bother him any, we'll all be busy with our goddamn lists." I swooped up my pile of notebooks and pictures off the end of his desk and stomped out the door.

I wasn't very far down the hall when he caught me. He can still move pretty fast. His big hand gripped my shoulder, and his voice said, very quietly, next to my ear, "Wait a minute."

We stood facing each other in the busy hall, both breathing a little fast and immediately aware that we looked ludicrously like a pair of teenagers in a lovers' quarrel.

"Shit, Jake," Frank said. "Come on and let's get some work done. That phone call made me mad. I'm sorry."

I shrugged and we both laughed, awkwardly. We went back in his office. Frank grabbed a pot of coffee and poured us each a cup.

"Let's look at pictures first," I said, and then to cover my embarrassment at having said that dirty word so soon again, I got busy adjusting lights and window shades to get illumination without glare. I showed him the complete set of Wahler prints, then cleared them away and laid out all the LaPlante pictures.

"You see what I mean?" I asked him. "How carefully it's all arranged? These are not smash-and-grab killings, Frank. There's no evidence of hurry or accident at either crime scene. Nothing that spells anger or passion. And no indication of a struggle. Now—" I took away the LaPlante set, then selected four prints, two from each set, that I thought showed traces of wheel marks, and put them side by side in front of him. I pointed over his shoulder, asking, "You see here—and over here—couldn't these be traces of wheel prints from a two-wheeler?"

I read him my transcription of Anne Condon's interview.

"I know her," Frank said. "I remember their store. You're right, she's a totally credible witness."

"All right," I said. "If we believe her story about what she saw, doesn't it seem likely that what you see in these pictures are the remnants of two-wheeler tracks that the murderer tried to brush out before he left? Remember, he's working in the dark."

"Possible, anyway. Let's say, for now, possibly these are wheel tracks. But then where are we going with this story? A man gets killed someplace else, we don't know where. His killer puts him on a two-wheeler, puts the two-wheeler in a truck. Brings him to a public park in the middle of the night, puts him in a softball uniform, chops pieces off his body, arranges this mutilated body in an obscene pose, and leaves him there?" He stared intently at the far wall, pulling at his nose. After a minute he cleared his throat, moved his shoulders uncomfortably, and protested, "It's so . . . elaborate. It seems so unnatural. Why would anybody . . . To send a *message*, you keep saying. A message saying what, Jake?"

"Put that aside for now," I urged him. "Do you agree the truck and the two-wheeler explain what we couldn't explain before, how the body could be there on the ground so neat with no sign of a struggle?"

"Oh, sure, that part. . . . He had to do all his cutting after he got to the site, though, right?"

"Yes. Otherwise there'd have been blood dripped all over the sidewalk, through the gate, and all along the path to the softball diamond, in Wahler's case, and likewise across the sidewalk and all over the grass from wherever he parked his truck at Willow Creek Park, in the LaPlante case. He'd never have been able to clean it all up, Frank, working in the dark the way we know he had to do.

"Now, admittedly, I don't have a time frame for the delivery of the second body yet. I haven't had time to find out if anybody in the Willow Creek neighborhood sighted the truck. But at Pioneer Park, we can pinpoint the time fairly accurately. Harley and Vince logged a drive-by of the area between midnight and twelve-twenty. Mrs. Condon saw the delivery truck arrive sometime near twelve-thirty, and she thinks it left soon after one o'clock. At one-thirty, Harley and Vince drove by again and saw the gate open, and that's when they went in and found the body."

"Uh-huh. The time kind of worries me. It's pretty close, isn't it? To do all he had to do? Get the body and the cushions in there, arrange it, do the cutting—"

"And take the picture, remember, and pin it on. He had to take the picture after the body was arranged. Of course, we don't know for certain that there was only one man. He could have had help. Somehow . . . I can't seem to picture that; the whole thing feels like one man with one mission, to me. If the body was already in the uniform, on the two-wheeler, he could do it, I think. Just about. He could have had the cushions under the tarp with the body, too. He'd have to be a strong man, organized, who'd thought it through in advance, knew just what he wanted to do."

"Mrs. Condon was pretty sure it was a man she saw?"

"Right." I read that part of her interview to him again. "Now, the other interviews—" I gave him the scanty, mostly negative, results of four days of talking to everybody I could find. They covered a lot of paper, but they didn't take us far. Frank was already glancing at the clock. It was nearly eight.

"Let me summarize what I've got from autopsies," I said. "You understand, DNA results won't be back for several days, and the second set of BCA test results won't come back till Monday, toxicity, hair and fiber, dirt comparisons, all that. But whatever else BCA is able to come up with won't change the fact that both bodies show definite evidence of strangulation. . . ." I laid it out for him.

"So on the basis of what you've got now, we have these strong similarities. Both victims strangled, no evidence they died of anything else. Both bodies mutilated after death. Strong suspicion the genitals in the second victim's mouth came from the first victim's body. And both bodies dressed up in this apparently meaningless softball player's getup that doesn't seem to signify anything because they didn't play ball, nobody can seem to remember that they ever played ball."

"No. Well, LaPlante did, in high school. His mother's looking for a picture of him in his uniform then. But not since then, and that would be, what, four or five years ago."

"Uh-huh. What have you got that connects the two of them, then? They work together, drinking buddies, what?"

"Well, that's the hell of it, Frank. So far, they don't connect to softball and they don't seem to connect to each other. I asked the LaPlantes, did Wahler come to the house, was he somebody your son mentioned? They don't remember ever meeting or seeing him. I asked Vince just now; he says he saw LaPlante frequently after local sports events and doesn't ever remember seeing Wahler till he found him dead. I haven't had time to call Tammy Wahler yet." Frank saw my little wince, and grinned.

"Be careful how you ask her," he said.

"I'll give her plenty of space," I said. "Also, remember Ace Barber, our deadbeat dad? I've got a guy in St. Paul helping me, trying to match up mutilation crimes, in the three states that are after him, with the periods of his residence in those states. And I lifted two pieces of junk mail out of his wastebasket, on the strength of that warrant I had, and I'm having them tested for prints. If we get anything, I'll get St. Paul to put 'em in their computer and try for a match with anything we got from the Wahler crime scene. I really don't like him for these crimes at all, but I figured I had to check it out. One trap I'm trying to avoid, Frank, is getting too set on the idea that these crimes have only one perp. We could have one originator and a copycat."

"Okay. But if the Barber lead doesn't pan out, Jake, you hand off the follow-up to one of the other detectives, hear? We want to cooperate with other states on these deadbeat cases, but for now I want you concentrated on these two murders and nothing else."

"Right," I said. The clock said twenty minutes to nine. "About the FBI, Frank, can we put that decision off till Monday? Can't do anything about it today anyway. And I'd rather talk about my list of questions."

Frank drank the last of his coffee and stared at the bottom of the mug. "Yes. Wait. Let me ask one first. Did the schools come up with any promising leads to the equipment?"

"No. Oh, and I just remembered that, good thing you asked. Andy Dornoch says I can see his lost-and-found Monday, but I haven't had an answer to my question about midnight deliveries to the park. I'm gonna call him at home," I said, making a note, "as soon as I get outta here, and find out about that."

"Oh, I'll see Andy at this Elks Lodge event at Bryant Field. He told me some time ago he'd be handling the loud-speaker equipment. I'll remind him to call you. Okay, shoot, first question."

"Okay. Assume for the sake of argument that Anne Condon saw the killer at Pioneer Park Monday night, and not just some deliveryman. Why did he lock the gate behind him when he went in, but leave it standing open when he came out?"

"He forgot," Frank said. "He was in a hurry."

"Maybe. But he seems so organized, so cool. He locked

the gate when he went in, to ensure that he wouldn't be disturbed while he did his business, right? Why wouldn't he take the same care to lock it again on the way out? Or at least close it. If he'd even closed it, Greeley and Mundt would have assumed it was locked like before. Then the body probably wouldn't have been discovered till morning, like the second one. But by leaving the gate standing wide open—it was almost as if he wanted to be sure somebody would find it earlier. But why? Why would he care?"

"See what you mean. Something about time—a better time for finding a body? Huh. No time's convenient for finding dead guys, in my experience. . . . I'm drawing a blank on that one, Jake."

"Second question, Why does he take the picture?"

"For kicks. What else?"

"Maybe. Think of it, though. A picture taken with a flashbulb in the middle of the night in a darkened public space . . . it increases the risk of discovery enormously. Kind of hard to see how it could add to the fun. Unless for some reason it's a necessary part of what he's trying to do."

"Really, I think you're trying to be too logical, here, Jake," Frank said. "If the guy's a freak, who's killing people for thrills, we can't be expected to understand him. I mean, describe his behavior, sure, match it to a pattern if we can. But we can't expect to understand his motivation like we'd understand each other. Forget about understanding. We just have to catch him."

"Yeah, but look at the organization and the—I'm tempted to say, the *hard work* that's gone into what he's done so far. You have to give him this: a guy who gets his victims into a costume, dresses them up and stands them on a two-wheeler in a truck, and moves them around to where he wants them to be, he's going to a lot of trouble, Frank. He isn't just bashing and slashing at random, this is no mad dog running amok. He's trying, on some very painstaking way to say . . . *something* . . . and the pictures have to be part of that. So I think we should consider what they could be saying."

"Which is what?"

"I have no idea," I said, and Frank laughed sharply and said, "Swell. How many more of these brilliant questions you got? I gotta leave here in five minutes without fail."

"One more. Where's the hand?"

"The what?"

"The hand, Frenchy LaPlante's hand."

The chief rocked his big chair back on its springs so hard it squealed and fixed me with his pale blue glare. "They still haven't found his hand? It wasn't around there anyplace in the park? You sure?"

"Three squads searched all yesterday morning while we were guarding the space. And we put it in on the afternoon duty list, for every car that had any free task time. Willow Creek Park and the two blocks around it have been gone over inch by inch, quite thoroughly. The hand wasn't there."

Frank stared dismally out the window.

"Shit," he said softly. "So you think . . . ?"

"It figures, doesn't it?" I said. "The hand is for the next guy."

Frank punished the springs on his chair for a couple of minutes. Suddenly he smashed his fist hard into a pile of papers in the middle of his desk. The crash startled me so much I almost fell out of my chair; papers flew all over, and he hurt his hand. He sat back with an aggrieved look, cradling his sore hand in his left armpit.

"Goddamn it, I hate this," he said. "I'm responsible, but I don't control anything. There's somebody out there that's calling all the shots, and we're not even close to knowing who he is or what he's going to do next. The one thing we know for sure is that we'll hate it when we do find out. And now I have to go and umpire a ball game? It feels like an absolutely ridiculous thing to do, but I promised, so I gotta go do it. *Shit.*" He stood up, straightened his clothes, took a couple of deep breaths, and finally said, "Yeah, well, see ya later."

He left me sitting there, cowed and miserable, and went charging out the door looking cross and dangerous as a grizzly bear. I hate being around him when he gets like this, but I did understand how he felt. He was furious about the information leak. And until we made substantial progress on these two murder investigations, he felt jumpy and defensive about being anyplace but the station. But he's never been able to say no to anybody, so he's doomed to run around like a nut all weekend, umpiring games, passing out prizes, and toting potato salad. Besides getting exploited by every civic do-gooder within a hundred miles, he's on call to his wife and five kids, and both his parents, and about a hundred McCafferty relatives. Monday morning saves his life every week; seven straight days of Frank's weekends would kill anybody.

Usually he seems to thrive on being indispensable. But the way he looked this morning, I devoutly hoped none of the youth of Rutherford decided to question any of his calls.

I went back to my office and called Andy Dornoch at both his numbers. His secretary's recorded voice answered at Parks and Recreation, reminding me that the office was closed until Monday and inviting me to leave a message. When the beep sounded I said, "Andy Dornoch, goddammit, call Jake Hines this minute before you take another breath!" and hung up.

Ten rings on his home phone got me nothing but echoes. I felt frustration churning in my gut, so I took a deep breath and put him deliberately out of my mind. Frank would talk to him at the tournament, and he would call. I wanted to keep working through my chores, not bog down on any one item and not get involved in any more emotional issues. That's always the best way, in police work: keep slogging along. You turn over a hundred rocks and don't find any worms? Turn over another hundred. Or, harder still, go back and find that first hundred rocks, and turn those suckers over again.

·NINE·

I began calling the softball players on Lou Bjornson's list, looking for somebody who would establish a connection between Wahler and LaPlante, or remember Wahler playing softball. Out of ten phone calls, I reached six team members, pretty good luck for a Saturday. But nobody remembered seeing the two men together, and they were all firm about never having seen Wahler in a game.

I started getting that swampy feeling that's so hard to fight, when none of my ideas work and I feel as if I'm doomed to flail around in a sinkhole till some cloudburst does me a favor and drowns me. All my phone calls took five or ten minutes longer than usual, too, because each person I talked to wanted me to reassure him that the police were making progress.

"Yeah, the wife's been after me," Delbert Pike said. "Just

yesterday she says to me, 'What kind of a town is this turning into, anyway?' she says, 'I don't know whether it's safe to let the kids play outside or not.' I didn't really now *what* to tell her." He vented a nervous little laugh, heh-heh-heh, so false it made my teeth ache. Then he transferred his panic back to his spouse, asking, "I mean, I guess she's got reason to be anxious, huh?"

I gave him my speech about families staying close and taking care, and I told him we'd announce all developments in a timely fashion. "Announcing developments in a timely fashion" is a piece of bureaucratic jargon I heard the DA use recently. It slid off my tongue in an oily, effortless way that kind of scared me, but I noticed that Pike seemed satisfied.

Jack Delaney cut right to the chase. "You going to catch this mad-dog killer pretty soon?"

"We certainly hope so."

"Well, hope, Jesus, is that all you got? I mean, suspects, have you got any suspects?"

"I'm not free to divulge details of the case, Mr. Delaney," I said, in my hymn-singing voice, "but the full resources of the department are being brought to bear on the investigation, rest assured."

"Full resources of the department" was one of Frank's new pet phrases. I saw now why he liked it; it's true, and it's meaningless.

It all takes time, though. My watch was a battery-powered digital, but it seemed to me I could hear it ticking.

Tammy Wahler, oddly subdued, said she didn't know LaPlante, "but that don't mean much, Jim didn't bring his drinking buddies home." I thought of telling her about the paycheck she probably had coming from Ace Barber. But it seemed pointless to give her one more thing to be mad about, so I let it go.

"Did you ever reach your husband's mother, Mrs. Wahler?" I asked her.

"Oh, yeah, she came for the funeral. Didn't she call you? I told her to. She left right from the church to go back to Baraboo, that's where she's living now. Her and me don't get along too good." Why was I not surprised? I asked for the senior Mrs. Wahler's address and phone number, and waited for a long time while Tammy dug it out of one of her piles.

Francine LaPlante whispered hello, remote as a ghost. Somebody must have given her tranquilizers without reading all the ingredients in her ongoing medication. She perked up a little when I reminded her why I was calling; she had gone through old family pictures and found one of Louis in his uniform. She wanted to tell me about some of the others she had found. I watched the seconds scroll across the face of my watch while she described, in that hollow half-speed voice, shots of Louis holding the first fish he ever caught, Louis with his confirmation class. Would I like to see those?

I told her I just wanted to see the team photo. I assured her, several times, that it was going to be a big help.

"Could I borrow it long enough to make copies?" I asked.

"All right," she answered, sounding more than ever as if she was speaking to me from deep in a hole. She must be dosed up with cough suppressant on top of her tranquilizers; she hadn't coughed at all while we were talking. There was an upside to her condition, though; her pharmaceutical cocktail was allowing her to deal with tragedy at arm's length.

"If I came by your house in a few minutes," I asked her, wishing I didn't have to do it, "could I pick up that picture? I'll take it straight to the developer and have it back to you by Monday."

"That'll be fine," she croaked, with an eerie pause between each syllable.

I called Jay Billingsley to beg him for a quick weekend turnaround. He said he'd just come in from photographing nesting mallards on the river and intended to spend the weekend developing pictures anyway. "Bring it over as soon as you can," he said, "and then don't bother me again till Monday morning, and you got a deal."

I hung up and sat staring down at the calls I had logged; twelve in two hours. Who next? Just then my phone rang, and Frank yelled, above the din of many juvenile voices, "Jake? Listen, first chance I had to call you. Andy Dornoch's not here, we had to set up the PA system without him. And he doesn't answer his home phone. Maybe you ought to send a car by his house, see if he's okay."

"Aw, listen," I said, wishing Frank didn't always have to stew about every little thing. "Andy probably got some hot new okra seeds, just got working in his yard and spaced out the Elks Lodge entirely. But tell you what, I'm heading out to do errands in a couple of minutes, I'll go by and check on him myself."

It was almost lunchtime anyway. I trotted down the silent Saturday stairs, plotting my next four moves. I would go get Mrs. LaPlante's picture and take it to Jay Billingsley. Then I would drive to Andy Dornoch's house and get him to answer my two simple questions, about his lost-and-found bin and his deliveries. Immediately after that conversation, I would drive to the root beer stand on North Broadway and get a double order of tacos and refried beans from a carhop. I would sit outside, sleepily content in brilliant sunshine, eating spicy food and drinking root beer, looking down with satisfaction at Dornoch's answers, written neatly in my steno pad.

"You can see my lost-and-found bin Monday morning at X hour," it would say, "and yes, the whosis company delivers the whatsis every Monday night," or, "No, we have never had anything delivered in the middle of the night, what a dumb idea, why would we do that?" One way or the other, I could digest my lunch in peace and go on to the next step. Which was what? Reading from the FBI list of serial killings, I decided, but I'll be damned if I'll think about it until after the second taco.

The LaPlante house was full of women, cooking, answering the phone, and thanking each other for casseroles delivered to the kitchen door. I started salivating while I rang the doorbell; the whole house smelled like fried chicken and chocolate cake. A woman with iron blue hair, wearing a printed cotton apron over a polyester pants suit, opened the door an said, "Oh, honey, we aren't buying anything at all today."

I held up my badge and stated my business. She squinted up at me with her head cocked like the little red hen, absorbing this odd information.

"Well, for heaven's sake, you people are getting onto the police force now, are you? Well, I suppose that might be a good idea in the long run, if it keeps you from—well, here, come on in." She led me across the living room, saying in the hushed tones people reserve for death and disgrace, "Francine? Hon? Mr. Haynes to see you?"

They had enthroned her in the best chair. It was obviously her husband's, a big recliner covered in some stiff, slidy fabric, and she had trouble staying erect in it. Uncomfortably marooned on her tweedy island, she alternated between clutching the armrests and bracing her feet against the hassock.

She was enjoying the attention, though, and she was glad to see me. Smiling up mistily through her Prozac haze, she clutched my right hand in both of hers. We shook interlocked hands for some time, making little soft sounds. Her neighbor, my guide, beamed down upon us, like a hostess whose party is going well.

Francine loosened her grip eventually, to pick up the five-year-old Hillside High School annual she had ready on the table beside her. She opened it to a back page filled with photos of athletic teams and held it up to me proudly. Tears leaked out from behind her smeary glasses and trickled slowly down her face as she pointed out a younger, slimmer Louis, in the middle of the second row. I wouldn't have recognized him.

"Let's see," I said, counting across the row quickly so I wouldn't lose him, "he's fifth from the left in the middle row."

"Well, yes," she said, "but if you lose track, the names are listed under the picture. See, here he is." Looking down obediently where she pointed, I read across the line that said "Second row," found LaPlante's name, and then realized I had just read another name I recognized. It was next to his, on the left. I looked back and read it again: James Wahler.

So there it was. They did know each other once, in high school, and the connection was softball. Counting again, across the second row in the picture, I found Wahler, a skinny kid grinning in a too-large uniform, just to LaPlante's left.

"Mrs. LaPlante," I asked, trying to keep the excitement out of my voice, "do you remember this boy, James Wahler? Next to your son on the left?"

She looked at him indifferently, her eyes vague. "No, I don't believe I do."

I couldn't see much resemblance, myself, to the red, puffy face I remembered from Pioneer Park. But Tammy would be able to confirm that this was her husband, surely, even if he was a couple of years younger in the picture than he had been when she met him. If Tammy wasn't sure, I'd get his mother to identify the picture. I could probably locate the coach from that year, too. Satisfaction swelled inside me like a balloon. As soon as I put Wahler and LaPlante together on that team for sure, I had tied them together through softball. I felt certain that was going to put me a big step closer to the reason for their deaths.

Francine put the old yearbook in a plastic sack and handed it over to me reluctantly, after I repeated my assurances that I'd get it back to her Monday morning. The same unctuous woman led me out, as though I might not be able to find the front door I had just come in through. I thanked her as generously as if she had just pulled me into a boat in a flood.

I got behind a Heart Fund Bike-a-thon during the drive from LaPlante's house to Jay's shop, so what should have been a five-minute drive took fifteen. Jay's assistant said they couldn't possibly do my work over the weekend. I opened my mouth to protest, but Jay stuck his head out of a rear door and said, quickly, "It's okay, Ellie, just leave it, Jake," and disappeared again. Ellie rolled up her eyes, and I shrugged. Whaddaya gonna do, our shared smile said, he's a photographer.

"Six copies, please," I said, and clipped my receipt carefully in my steno pad. You never know at Jay's shop; his Monday assistant might claim to have no record of my order. He's always in a cash crunch, so he employs part-time helpers who sometimes seem to be trying to master telephone dialing. At the drugstore you get system; Jay's running on passion.

I'd never been to Dornoch's house, but I knew where it was. Rutherford's an easy town to navigate; it grew up along a north-south river, so it's pretty much aligned with the compass, and most of the street names follow numbered sequences. Andy's address was 1923 Eighteenth Avenue Southwest. I followed Tenth Street to the golf course, made a dogleg to Fourteenth, and turned west on Eighteenth Avenue.

When my bride and I were shopping for our first home, which also turned out to be our last home, I tried to persuade her to look at the houses in this neighborhood. Nancy wanted something newer. It's just as well; if we'd owned a house on Eighteenth Avenue, I'd probably have fought her for it.

They're mostly twenties-vintage homes, built to their owners' specifications. They have things nobody even thinks of asking for anymore, like window seats and pantries, and they've been lovingly tended, often by several generations of the same family. The serene good looks of each house is augmented by the tidy solidarity of its neighbors. Not lavish but comfortable, they have classic Minnesota charm: big yards, huge trees, porches with swings.

Andy's house had two stories and an attic with dormers. It was on a corner lot, with a hydrangea hedge across the front, and lilac bushes blooming down the Twentieth Street side. There was a two-car garage on that side, with both doors closed. Andy's car was sitting on the cement apron in front of one of the closed doors.

I rang the bell; it sounded in the house, but nothing stirred. I tried the front door; it was unlocked. Hesitantly I opened the heavy door, stuck my head in the dark-paneled front hall, and called, "Andy?" The silent house rebuked my intrusion.

He had to be out back. His car was in the drive. I followed a neat walk along the side of the house, where tulips and daffodils bloomed. I saw a rose garden ahead. Beyond it, a wheelbarrow full of dirt stood beside a freshly dug vegetable patch. There was a spade stuck in the dirt, and a canvas sack of tools nearby.

He had added a wooden deck to the back of his house, with a barbecue setup just outside the kitchen door. I climbed four steps onto the deck, calling, "Andy?" Nobody answered. I walked to the railing; I could see the whole backyard from there.

I saw his feet first, under a tree. It was one of those monster oaks, several stories tall, that often dominate old Minnesota yards. Birds and squirrels were nesting all over it, and a wooden table and bench circled its base. I could see the remnants of a tree house on one of the lower branches.

Andy was wearing old green twill pants—serious work pants—and high-laced farmer's shoes. I called, louder, "Andy?" stood still in puzzlement for a few seconds when he didn't answer, and then finally saw, with a suffocating rush of blood away from my heart, that his feet were not quite touching the ground.

I made two jumps off the deck and sprinted across the lawn to his side. But I could see right away that there was no hurry. The dark red, distorted face of Andy Dornoch swung from a rope, a couple of feet above my head.

I touched his cheek. It was cold and rigid, and his jaw was set. His eyes looked flat and milky, and his skin had taken on the waxy look of the dead.

My lungs seemed to have quit working. I heaved desperately, trying to suck in air. The world whirled and went dark, with red edges. I clamped my hands on the sides of my face and screamed soundlessly. That broke the airlock, and the scenery steadied down.

A six-foot wooden ladder lay on its side nearby. He must have climbed it and jumped off. Knocked it down when he jumped. Terrible way to hang yourself; not enough room, not enough height. He probably didn't even break his neck. He had to hang there, kicking, till he ran out of air. The length of the rope had to be just right, too, to give him the maximum drop, but not let him reach the ground. He must have stood out here and measured it carefully. Goddamn. Did you use that little metal tape you always carry, Andy? I got a distinct mental image of him, alone in his beautiful yard, with his tulips and roses around him, preparing the instrument of his death.

I ran to my car, gulped a couple of breaths so my voice wouldn't wobble, grabbed my radio mike off its hook, and called the station.

Cunningham said, "You want the respirator unit, Jake?"

"It's no use," I said, "he's cold and stiff, he's been dead for some time. Let's see, it's Saturday, the Hampstead County lab is closed. And Pokey won't be in his office. . . . Best thing to do is call the emergency room at Methodist Hospital, Tom, that way we'll get a doctor to certify cause of death, and an ambulance for transport. Might as well tell them, though, no need to hit the siren and come speeding out here. This is DOA for sure. And listen, after you call the hospital, you can try to reach Pokey at home, but if he's not there just leave a message."

I turned around from hanging up my mike, and Frank was there.

"Frank," I said, "how'd you get here so fast?"

"So fast after what?" he said. "What's going on?" I put my hand on his arm. It felt like holding a fencepost. "Dornoch's hung himself in his backyard," I said.

He made an awful sound and pulled away from my hand, running head long past the house, destroying tulips, kicking a watering can aside. When I caught up to him, he had his knife out and was sawing at the rope.

"Help me!" he yelled.

"Frank!" I grabbed his arms from behind and shook as hard as I could. It was like trying to shake a tree. "Look at him, for Christ's sake!" Frank gave me a crazy look, and for a second I thought he was going to hit me. Then reason came back into his eyes. He let the knife drop and took a couple of raspy breaths. Then he touched the corpse quietly and looked at the curled blue fingers.

"Aw, Andy," he said sadly, to the pitiful figure suspended there. He turned to me and whispered, "Jesus, Jake, isn't this just the *shits*?"

"Yes," I said, "it is. But leave him alone now till the ambulance crew gets here. We need somebody to certify cause of death."

"Yeah, you're right." He shook his head a few times, mournfully. Finally he took a long, deep breath and asked, in his usual voice, "What about pictures? You got your camera?"

I was getting it out of my car when Stearns and Donovan arrived. Cunningham had sent them to see if I needed help. I shot a roll of film before the ambulance arrived, and while Stearns and Donovan were helping them get the body down, Casey and Longworth arrived. Within five minutes, eight more blue-and-white squad cars crowded in around Andy Dornoch's corner. Frank took charge, posting a squad front and back and getting a third pair busy taping the scene. Everybody else he sent back on patrol. "Christ," he said, when the ninth car arrived, "who's watching the store?"

Pokey got there while the doctor from Methodist Hospital was examining the body, on a gurney in the yard. They noted temperature, rigor, and lividity, examined the bruises left on Dornoch's neck by the rope, and agreed to transport the body to the hospital morgue for the weekend. Pokey said he'd schedule an autopsy at the lab Monday morning.

"I just found him hanging from a tree in his yard," I said. "How much cause of death do you need?"

"Law says I gotta confirm," he said, squinting up at me in the noisy hard. The DA had arrived, and a couple of vans from the TV and radio stations. "You getting kinda fed up with all this dying stuff, Jake?" I turned away from his shrewd little pinched face, so wise from his many trips to hell and back.

"We don't usually bunch 'em up like this," I said.

"Oughta make new rule, probably," Pokey said, "guys wanna off themselves, least they can do is pick slower week."

"Damn straight," I said, but my smile felt stiff.

Then Parks and Recreation people began coming by to see if they could help, along with the off-duty cops, and city employees from other departments. Dornoch had worked for the municipality of Rutherford for over twenty years and been director of Parks and Recreation for almost ten. Everybody owed him favors. When his peers learned they'd been working with this helpful, cheerful guy who was secretly hurting so much that he'd decided to hang himself in his yard, they began to feel like insensitive clods. To absolve themselves, they came to his house and stood around in the way.

The block filled up with teachers, scout leaders, coaches, United Way execs, Head Start tutors, and AIDS March organizers. They clustered in anxious clumps, in the yard first and then spilling out into the street and down the block, telling each other how if they'd only known, they would have done anything, absolutely anything, my God, Andy was just such a helluva swell guy, you know? Frank went into crowd-control mode and began appealing to people to move out. It was touchy work, and it took a long time, because these were all friends, not strangers. And while they were obstructing traffic in the neighborhood, so were most of the neighbors. It was a surreal scene, clusters of distressed people wearing T-shirts with silly slogans on them, holding on to each other and keening softly, crying on their running shoes, loaning each other scruffy wads of Kleenex dug out of their shorts.

As soon as Pokey took charge of the body, Frank told me, "I'm gonna assign Anderson to be the detective in attendance at this autopsy, Jake. This is a suicide, it's got nothing to do with the cases you're working on, and you've got enough to do without it."

"Good by me," I said. "Anything more I can do for you?"

"Hell, no," Frank said, "I got enough cops here for a firefight. Why don't you go on back to what you were working on? If you can remember what it was, can you?" He looked at me with some concern; I must have been showing a little wear and tear.

"No problem," I said. Like everybody else, I tend to say, "No problem" just as problems spin completely out of control. I got in my car, dug out my phone book, and looked up Jay Billingsley's number. He answered after eleven rings, sounding exasperated. When I said my name he said, "Jake, you *promsied*—"

"You won't believe this," I said, "but I just took pictures of another dead body."

"Shit, Jake. Maybe I should just nail my door shut, I don't feel safe on the street any more. What the hell has gone wrong with this town?"

"I dunno. But could you possibly do one more set of pictures?"

He thought a minute. "Okay," he finally said. "If you'll do something for me. I don't have anybody to help in the shop Monday, and I'm gonna be dead meat from working all weekend. Will you come by and get your pictures Sunday night? I'm gonna close up Monday and just put a sign on the door."

"You got it, buddy," I said. "Thanks."

Traffic was badly snarled as far south as Twentieth Avenue, but once out of that two-block area it was as though the hullabaloo in Dornoch's yard never happened. The rest of Rutherford dreamed on through a golden afternoon. The tennis courts were full. Homeowners were raking and clipping and planting all along the street. My watch said one-thirty. Could that be right? It felt like a couple of days since I had parked in front of Dornoch's house.

Jay's assistant wrote up my order without a word; evidently he had come out of his burrow long enough to tell her I was coming. I stapled the receipt alongside the earlier one, and we wished each other a great weekend, like old pals.

I headed back downtown toward the station, trying to get my brain sorted out. What *had* I been going to do after I saw Dornoch? I had a vague recollection of working my way through a list. Wait, was it records? I was getting ready to evaluate some records. Why? Then I remembered: the list of serial murders from the FBI.

"Fine. Swell. Super keen." A nice long list of serial murders. Such an original answer to the question of how to spend a beautiful Saturday afternoon in the glorious month of

May: crouch down in a dim little cubicle in a stuffy building and comb through old records of unspeakable crimes. What could possibly be more appropriate, when you've just finished photographing one of your colleagues dangling from a rope in his yard? Then maybe, on the way home tonight, just for the sake of consistency, I could get attacked by birds.

Wallowing in self-pity got me halfway back to the station before I remembered I still owed myself lunch. I couldn't face tacos at the drive-in, the pleasure I'd been planning before I found Andy Dornoch. I just stopped at a Wendy's and played that salad bar game where you see how many calories you can possibly pile on top of lettuce. I believe I may have topped my previous personal best.

·TEN·

AT THE DEPARTMENT, THE TELEPHONE CONSOLE WAS crackling with traffic. Word of Dornoch's suicide had spiraled outward from Eighteenth Avenue, spreading alarm and confusion. All along the path of the rumor, Rutherford householders were calling the station, hoping for a denial. As soon as the distressing news was verified, most of them added a second question, pretty much along the lines of, "What is this town coming to, anyway?" Tom Cunningham and his support staff were keeping up with the heavy telephone traffic okay, but dealing with the high anxiety was tough. They were using every one of the counseling skills they'd learned in Psych 101, layering on reassuring words and quiet, soothing tones of voice. They were probably all going to go home tonight and kick the cat.

I waved, got a couple of distracted nods in reply, and

scuttled into my office, which on second thought didn't seem all that unattractive. "No, ma'am, I really don't believe there's any reason why you should cancel your family reunion," I heard Cunningham say in his most reasonable voice as I stepped inside. With the door closed, the chatter went away.

Tom Eckert's fax was waiting for me, a thick fanfold of apparent serial crimes, nationwide. They were strings of killings, with similarities so striking they were presumed to have been perpetrated by one person, or possibly, the appended note pointed out, one perpetrator and one or two imitators. Jesus. Imitators. Like Rich Little doing John Wayne.

Since no killer had been positively identified in any of these series, all were considered ongoing, though some had been inactive for several years. Tom's note acknowledged that he had made no finds involving softball gear, but directed me to the section involving mutilations.

I settled down to read, beginning with the cases Tom had marked. The first set of killings had plainly targeted prostitutes, so I ruled it out. A second set, in which the victims were all boys and young men, held my attention for some time. But all the victims exhibited clear signs of anal intercourse before, during, and even after death. Since neither of my victims had been sodomized, I marked that set "unlikely."

One string of murders, through the south-central states, had been labeled "the Play-School Murders" by the tabloids, because the bodies had all been posed the way little girls pose their dolls: sitting on a chair at a table, or propped up in bed with toys. Three of the Play-School

Murders had occurred within the last year and a half, so the killer appeared to be still active.

For a few minutes, I considered the possibility that the Play-School Murders, and my two victims as well, might be laid at the movable doorstep of Ace Barber. But I had gathered substantial evidence that placed Ace and his roofing business in Iowa and Michigan near the times when the last three murders on the printout list were committed, in Texas and Louisiana. Considering Ace Barber's limited finances and battered pickup, that much fast travel looked like a stretch.

I read back and forth in the series, my hopes going up and down. None of the victims had been put into a costume, nor had the killer made any use of sports paraphernalia. Several victims had been female, too, and the mutilations performed on them indicated a fixation with mammaries. Still, the posing aspect held my attention. I highlighted the names and phone numbers of the investigating personnel in the three most recent states. I could call them on Monday. At least I'd be talking to guys who'd been consulting some of the same sources I had; maybe they could save me some time.

At first, I had to force myself through the reading. I conducted a quiet dialogue with the ugliness of the material, muttering, "Oh, for Christ's sake," and, "Ah, shit," twisting around in my chair and making faces at it. The list was poorly printed, on flimsy fax paper, fanfolded into a slippery pile; a couple of times I dropped it and had to pick the whole smeary mess up off the floor and put it back in order before I could go on. My reluctance to read through the sordid contents compounded my aggravation with the paper it was printed on; I was basically at war with the entire task.

After half an hour it began to get more routine, and by the second hour I was having trouble keeping my mind on it. The relentless narrative of evil took on a deadening banality. Many of the medical terms were only partly comprehensible to me. And several investigators seemed to think they could make the information more palatable by writing their reports in psychobabble about "stereotypical behaviors" (when did "behavior" get pluralized?) and bureaucratic jargon about "agent/vector factors." These show-offs just layered boredom and confusion on top of the other horrors I had to confront. Forced to read phrases like "parameters of opportunity" and "reliable markers for sociopathology," my brain turns into a mouse and begins digging an escape tunnel.

When I realized that I had been staring at the same section of the report for five minutes while actually planning a rock garden, I folded the paper carefully open at the account of the second Houston outrage, marked it with a paper clip, and reached my mug down from the bookshelf. Maybe more coffee would help.

I had my hand on the doorknob when the telephone rang.

"Jake?" the chief said, in an odd strangled voice. "Is that you?"

"Last I knew," I said. "What's up?"

"Can you come back out here to Dornoch's house right now, please?"

"Well . . . sure. What do you . . . you want me to bring anything or . . . ?"

"No. Just come right now without talking to anybody."

"Right." Plainly, Frank was in no mood to chat.

Keilly and Forbes were walking foot patrols, front and back, at Dornoch's house. "Chief said tell you he's in the kitchen," Keilly said, looking harassed. He hustled on down the sidewalk to move a carload of gawkers along. I went in through the dark, cool front hall. The living room was on my right, the dining room on my left, past the stairway. A swing door at the far end of the dining room led to a pantry, and then to the kitchen. Frank was standing by the sink, wearing plastic gloves. His face looked flushed and sore, as if he'd been scalded.

"We found Dornoch's brother in LaCrosse," he said, without preamble. "I told him Dornoch was dead. Explained to him about Andy's wife, Loretta, being in the hospital. Told him there was nobody but him to take charge of the house, see about a funeral, all that stuff. He said of course he'd come over, but he's got a small business and a big family, and it might take two or three days to make arrangements. So I promised him I'd look after the house till he could get here.

"I started through, locking windows, checking faucets. Thought I better see there's nothing spoiling in the refrigerator." His voice cracked. "Opened this thing up—" He strode to the big upright and flung open the two sides, refrigerator and freezer, at once. The interior was spotlessly clean and white. The few food items inside didn't come close to filling it. So it was easy for me to see that only one item lay on the second shelf on the freezer side.

"It's a hand," I said.

"Of course it's a hand, goddammit," Frank said. "Is it the one you've been looking for?"

"Oh . . . well . . . how could it . . . God, Frank, you think?"

"You tell me," Frank said, impatiently. "Does it look like the other one?"

I'm no good, it turns out, at assessing the appearance of hands that have been severed from their owners. It's harder than you might think. In the first place, I didn't want to look at it any longer.

"Please, Frank," I said, "close the door a minute." We faced each other in the dark, cool kitchen, across the gleaming brick-patterned tile floor and neat pine cupboards.

"Why would Dornoch have Frenchy LaPlante's hand in his freezer?" I pleaded. "That doesn't make any sense at all."

"Why would he have anybody's?" Frank asked. "So is it LaPlante's, or isn't it?" His relentless blue stare bored holes in my face while a grandfather clock, somewhere in the house, clicked loudly over and began to boom the hour. It was four o'clock.

"I can't be sure," I said, against a rising feeling of certainty, "until we get the lab open and compare it to the one on LaPlante's body."

"Do it," Frank said. "Call the station, get them to find somebody's home number, get a doc down there to open up for us."

I made the call. On an impulse, then I called Pokey's house. His wife said he was working in the yard. I waited while his quick, hard footsteps pounded toward the phone. I asked him if he'd care to come down and have a look. "Is Pope Catholic?" he asked, adding, in a disgusted, irrelevant aside, "Stupid quack grass always gonna win in this yard anyway."

"Congratulations," I said, "now you know everything the natives know about lawn care."

We all converged on the Hampstead County lab within a few minutes. Frank and I sat in the front seat of his car until Jason Stuart arrived. We had the hand between us, in a clear plastic baggie, and neither one of us wanted to stand around a parking lot holding it.

Once we got inside, it only took three minutes to establish, to everybody's satisfaction, that the hand from Dornoch's freezer looked just like the one on Louis LaPlante's body. It was pale and fat-fingered, with black hair growing thick across the back, down to the first knuckle joint, and broken, dirty fingernails. Pokey and Stuart were satisfied with the matchup in wounds, where the hand and wrist went together.

"Gotta prove it, though," Frank said. "Is a blood test enough?"

"Good for starts," Jason Stuart said, "if there's any ambiguity we'll do a DNA test."

"Okay," I said, "and I'm calling BCA right now, to ask for a crew to come down here Monday morning and help us with Dornoch's autopsy."

Pokey looked put out. "What we need that Chang kid for? Looks pretty routine to me."

"A zillion good pictures," I said, dialing, "and more DNA tests, if we need them. And hair and fiber tests, which might start to be worth their weight in gold now. Something to put Dornoch at the scene of those two killings—"

A young-sounding person named Lee answered the phone. I couldn't decide if the voice was male or female, and the name offered no clue. It made me realize how much of my phone personality is gender-specific; I started out warm and winning and shaded off toward hearty and collegial. It was all wasted on Lee, who reacted to a third request for assistance from Rutherford like somebody hearing about sliced bread for the first time.

"Wow, this is terrific!" Lee crowed. "Boy, wait'll Chang hears this, he's gonna shit a *brick*!"

"Uh-huh. Can we confirm for Monday morning at nine, then, Lee?"

"Oh, you bet. We'll make certain there's a van sitting right here, loaded and ready to go. Jimmy would never speak to me again if I let anything screw up his chance to get in on another Rutherford call. Come to think of it, he's in the building now, you want to hold on a minute?" I didn't, particularly, but Lee had already clicked off. I sat through some sappy elevator music for forty-five seconds, and then Jimmy's voice said, "Jake? You got another mutilation murder, no kidding?"

"No," I said. "We've got what looked like a simple suicide by hanging till a few minutes ago. But now we've found some evidence that appears to link it to the first two murders. But there's no mutilation, Jimmy, no softball uniform, no picture on the body, none of that stuff. Just evidence that doesn't seem to make any sense. So what we've got here is a genuine *mystery*, do you like that?"

"God, yes," Chang said softly.

"Hair and fiber, Jimmy, think hair and fiber. A lot more blood typing. Maybe another DNA test, bring a kit. Dirt samples. We need a common thread. Something that puts some one person at the site of all three deaths. And about pictures, do you think you can get Trudy again? She did a heck of a job for us before," I said, using the truth deviously.

"Oh, Jake, pictures and fingerprints are really just routine, any competent technician will do just as well," Chang said, blissfully self-absorbed. "But okay, if you like I'll see if she's on duty Monday. And I'll see you at the lab there at what? Nine o'clock?"

I hung up and listened to Frank, in high gear on his phone, telling Cunningham to detail two more squads to Dornoch's house for a complete search.

"Plenty of gloves and bags, tell 'em," I heard him say, "and a van, and dusting gear. Bring another camera, plenty of film. Oh, and listen, make sure they check the batteries on their Streamlights. We'll be doing the basement, too, and it's gonna be dark in the yard before long." He hung up the phone, said, "Ready?" to me, and strode out to the car without looking back.

"Better get running shoes, Jake," Pokey called after me. He loves watching Frank in flat-out management mode.

Frank and I started in the garage as soon as we got back. It was scrupulously neat, the way you'd expect Dornoch's garage to be, with a jack and some tools hanging on their hooks on the wall. The stall in front of Dornoch's car was empty. The second stall was occupied by a dark blue hi-cube van, with signs on both sides of the cab that said, "Parks and Recreation, Rutherford, Minnesota."

"It fits the description Mrs. Condon gave me of the delivery truck," I told him. "Dark. Mudguards, and a lift gate." I flipped the heavy metal hasp across the back, pushed the vertical bolts up out of their sockets, and we each took one wide metal door and swung it open.

The truck bed was empty, except for a tall two-wheeled hand truck, fastened upright to the right-hand wall of the interior with canvas straps.

"It all seems to be falling into place," Frank said. "God damn. I still don't believe this."

"Let's take a look in those cupboards," I said, pointing to the far end of the garage. We closed up the truck and walked over. They were padlocked. We wasted a few minutes trying to jimmy the lock, till Frank said, "Oh, what the hell," took a tire iron down from the wall, and knocked the metal strip off the door.

A couple of shelves held paint cans and brushes, jars of nails and screws, a stack of drop cloths. Two flat cardboard boxes occupied the middle shelf. I pulled out the top one and lifted the cover. It held a couple of old striped softball uniforms. I slid the top shirt out of its plastic bag. Size medium. No name, front or back. It had that same stale smell I'd noticed on LaPlante's body.

"Does it match?" Frank asked.

"Looks the same to me," I said. "I've got pictures downtown to compare it to, and we'll have the other two back from Jimmy in a day or two. But yeah, I'd say it matches."

The second box held a beat-up fielder's glove and a pair of old leather softball shoes with metal cleats.

"Like the shoes on Wahler and LaPlante," Frank said.

"Yup."

The extra squads began arriving, with the van and pickup and about a ton of equipment. "Get these things bagged and tagged, will you?" Frank said. "I'm going to start one crew searching the house, and the other one digging up that vegetable patch."

Dornoch had measured out rows and marked them with stakes at each end. Waxed string was pulled taut between the stakes to keep the rows straight. On the rows he'd already planted, the brightly illustrated paper seed bags were shoved onto the stakes for reminders. Putratz and Hisey, good farmer's sons, stood reluctantly at the edge of the neat garden, holding their spades, till Frank said grimly, "Come on, guys, losing a few seeds isn't going to bother Dornoch today." Then they stacked stakes and string neatly at one side and started digging, but gingerly, as if time might reverse this nightmare and they'd be asked to put everything back to rights.

They found LaPlante's clothes first. They were just as his mother had described them: jeans, a blue T-shirt, a dark green windbreaker. Hisey's spade hit the tight ball, a couple of feet under the carrot seeds, and slid off. An electric difference seemed to come over the crew when he pulled the green jacket out of the hole. They quit feeling like marauders in a neat man's garden and turned into grim cops looking for evidence.

Even so, sunlight was long gone, and four of Rutherford's finest were sweating hard in the concentrated glare from three Streamlights, by the time they unearthed Wahler's stuff. It was on the opposite side of the patch, beneath the tomato seedlings. We didn't have a description of Wahler's outfit, but Dornoch had conveniently buried the victim's wallet along with his clothes. It wasn't going to be much help to Tammy, I saw; Wahler had been down to his last eleven bucks.

By then I'd gone back over the cargo van. There was a padlock in the glove compartment, alongside a late-model

Polaroid camera. The three-foot wire cable from the pad-lock was coiled up under the driver's seat.

Under the passenger's seat, I found a burlap bundle. I laid it on the hood of the truck and opened it carefully. It contained something heavy wrapped in white rags. Reluctantly, I unrolled the rags and found a hunting knife, cleaned and oiled.

"No blood on the knife," I said when I showed it to Frank. "Naturally Dornoch would clean his knife. I didn't see any on the rags either, but BCA might find something."

"Guess that kind of wraps it up," he said. "For tonight, anyway. Bag it and tag it. All this stuff. And then let's get it down to the station and call it a night. I'm gonna call Sheila and ask her to cook something. Wanna come eat with me?"

"Boy, do I," I said. I raced to the station to get my evidence checked in ahead of the digging crews.

Half an hour later, Sheila McCafferty set down a big blue platter, filled with bacon and eggs and potatoes enough for at least four sumo wrestlers, in the middle of the McCafferty kitchen table. Frank and I ate every morsel. We were too hungry for much conversation, which was just as well since the whole house vibrated with rap music, arguments, and phone conversations. Frank's kids are uninhibited.

We took our second beers out to the backyard, fished a couple of lawn chairs out of the clutter of bikes and sports equipment there, and sat in the fragrant dark, listening to the windows rattle. Frank shook his head.

"I swear it's all going to come down some day," he muttered.

He fiddled with a twig off his birch tree. Finally he said, "You believe this about Dornoch?"

"It doesn't seem real to me yet. But . . . we have to believe our eyes, I guess, don't we? that hand—and the buried clothes and all the rest of the stuff in the garage . . ."

"Uh-huh. I guess. I keep looking for some other explanation. It just doesn't fit with anything else I know about him."

"You known him a long time?"

"All my life, I guess," Frank said. "I've been trying to think. I certainly don't remember ever meeting him. He was always just there. We were never best friends or any of that. Just . . . we grew up in the same neighborhood, our parents knew each other a little, just to nod to. We were in the same Scout troup, once, and it seems to me we played on some of the same teams in school. I never paid particular attention to him. But yeah, he was always around."

A phone rang in the house; Sheila answered it and called up the stairs, "Katy?" A shrieking argument took place at the head of the stairs, followed by a great thumping of heels. Then Katy's voice, with the charm turned on full bore, caroled, "Hello? Oh, *hi!*"

"Katy's turning into a star," I said. Frank made a face.

"Tell me about it. Damn shame, too, she has the potential to be a really good basketball player." Frank's theories of parenting seem to center on vigorous team sports. He sat listening to his daughter's teasing laughter for a minute, then heaved himself out of his chair and went in to get us another beer. He said something to Katy in passing and got a vigorous head-shake and a very Frank-like glare in return. Back outside, he settled his big body into his creaking aluminum chair and groaned.

"Man, what a day, huh? Christ, I hope this is the end of

this mess. It's funny, though—all week I've been yelling at you for answers, just find me some answers. Now we have found some answers, and I swear I feel worse than ever. It just doesn't seem right. . . ." He stared into the blackberry bushes at the foot of his lawn, destroying turf under his chair with his big feet, and then turned toward me, his pale eyes staring anxiously in the reflected light from the kitchen window.

"I always had it a little easier than Andy, I guess," he said. "My dad was a cop, my family was always short on cash but we had the necessities. Dornoch's dad never seemed to have a steady job, and he drank some. Even in grade school, Andy was always working, after school, weekends, summers. He joined the Marines the week we graduated from high school. Served eight years. Did a tour in 'Nam, I think." Another silence. "He'd grown a lot when he came back, otherwise he seemed pretty much the same. Quiet— well, you know what he was like."

"Reasonable, I always thought. Had high standards for himself, but easy enough to work with."

"Exactly," Frank said. "Reliable—hell, you could set your clock by him, almost. He got that job with the city, got a little maroon Chevy coupe, you could see him going to work every morning at seven-forty-five exactly, back home for lunch at twelve-oh-five, and away again at twelve-fifty. Five days a week without fail. He got one of those plaques after ten years, for never missing a day."

A rattletrap sedan, with a bass-to-the max tape deck rattling the doors, pulled into the McCafferty driveway. The driver honked, and Andy McCafferty, sweater and sneakers flopping, flew out of the house. He exchanged four or five screamed insults with the occupants of the car, jumped in, and they roared off. The chief looked after them thoughtfully.

"Andy brought Loretta back to Rutherford with him when he came back from the marines. He'd met her while he was stationed at Camp Lejeune. Sweet girl. Seemed like they got along real well. They had a lot of trouble starting a family. Loretta lost three or four babies before she had Amanda. Mandy, they always called her. Pretty little thing. But she got kind of—oh, sort of demanding I guess you'd say, when she got older. Little bit spoiled, I suppose. Only natural. She just meant the world to them.

"In high school, she pretty much got out of control. Got in with a real wild bunch. And besides, she got into that dieting craze that some teenage girls start now, just wanted to be real thin. But she wanted to party too, and of course that combination's dangerous. In the spring of her senior year, it seemed like she just kind of—wilted. Quit going to school, laid in bed all day and wouldn't eat. They had to drag her out for treatment, and nothing worked. Anorexia nervosa, that's what the doctors told them. And that summer, one day while they were both at work, she took a lot of pills, a whole bottle of tranquillizers that the doctor had prescribed for her, and a bottle of aspirin besides. Wouldn't get up at all for dinner, but they were sort of used to that by then. Toward morning they heard her breathing funny and called an ambulance, but she flat-lined on the way to the hospital and they lost her.

"Andy took it hard of course, but Loretta, well, she never could seem to think about much of anything else after that. I suppose, being the mother, she blamed herself. She's never been a whole person since. This isn't the first time Loretta's had to be hospitalized. She just can't snap out of the depression.

"So—but—would that explain something like this, these two murders? You ever hear of such a thing before, Jake? A normal hard-working person like Andy Dornoch who gets pushed over the edge by bad luck and turns into a monster?"

"No," I said, firmly. "And when you put it that way, I don't believe a word of it, Frank. There has to be more—"

"What more? How do you mean?"

"I don't know." I stood up. "And I can't even guess at it tonight. I'm going to go in and kiss your wife, and thank her for the best meal I ever ate, and then I'm going to drive home, and hope to get there before I fall asleep."

"Oh, hey, do that. And listen, Jake, you take tomorrow off, you hear me? Go fishing, or play golf. I can't have you burning out on me. Nothing useful you can do on Sunday anyway. But then, Monday? I hate like hell to say this, but I think you oughta be at that autopsy with Pokey and them after all."

"Right. Agreed. All the same big pile of garbage now, isn't it?" I was halfway up the back steps when he called after me, "By the way, that Chang fella called this afternoon, and they put him through to me. He said to tell you that he did get Trudy Hanson assigned, for the fingerprints and pictures Monday morning."

"Oh, good," I said, without turning around, "that'll save some time."

After that I wasn't so sleepy anymore, so when I got home I called Ralph Noonin.

"Hey, Noons," I said, "Weather's supposed to be perfect tomorrow. Whaddaya say we float the boat?"

Ralph and I each own half of a seventeen-foot Lund Pro-V, which he keeps at his place because he's got a two-car garage and a tolerant wife.

"Your turn to buy the gas," Ralph said. He's an accountant, what can I say?

"Okay," I said, "so you're gonna bring lunch, right? And the beer—"

"I'll bring lunch," Ralph said, "and we can buy the beer at the Circle K next to the bait shop. You up for going early? Beat some of the traffic on the road—"

We thrashed out all of the tough decisions that go with fishing trips. I went right off to sleep then, after one more beer and the last half of an ancient detective movie starring Efrem Zimbalist Jr. Efrem solved the case by recalling a couple of lines from the victim's last book of poetry. Something to think about.

· ELEVEN ·

"GIMME TWO SCOOPS OF THOSE FATHEAD MINNOWS," Noonin said. The bait shop was already crowded, even though the sun was just above the trees. At the store next door we bought a twelve-pack and crushed ice, and two big cups of coffee to take along. Ralph insisted on buying the Sunday paper, too. I told him I didn't want any part of it, but after I got back in the car I managed to fish out the funnies without looking at the front page. He was busy swearing at traffic by then; Highway 63 was full of cars trailing aluminum boats like ours.

We launched at the first ramp on the south side of Lake City and motored east across Lake Pepin, which is a wide spot on the Mississippi created by the Alma Dam. Noons claims that walleye and sauger are more plentiful on the Wisconsin side of the Mississippi in May, and for all I know he may be right. My fishing technique has been picked up mostly from barroom bragging and the literature on the backs of tackle packages. I really have no idea why fish do what they do.

Ralph killed the outboard and let the boat drift while we baited up.

"How come you're fishing without a sinker, Jake?" he said, as I started stringing my minnow on the hook. "You got some new theory about where the fish are?"

"I'm not!" I said, "Am I? Aw, jeez—" I threw the bait back in the bucket and began untying the leader from the swivel. I groped around in my tackle box till I found the three-cornered lead sinker, strung it on the line, and reassembled the whole business. The first fishing trip of the year is always like this, for me; I spend the first hour or two trying to remember the little I know about fishing, including why I thought it was fun. Then I settle into it and never want to go home.

"I wouldn't think it was too surprising if you were just a tad distracted," Ralph said. "You've had quite a week with all this Hillside Strangler–type crime wave, haven't you?" He was hoping for some inside kinky stuff to tell the guys at work tomorrow, I could see. I didn't want to talk about it on my one day off, though, so I said, "Oh, you know, you get used to the way guts stink after a while," and after that he didn't ask me any more.

Ralph started the little trolling motor and settled himself on the high swivel seat forward, where he could control the motor with his foot. The sun was still low enough so that the trees on shore cast long shadows. We drifted through alternating patches of brightness and shade. One minute it'd be cool, almost chilly, then we'd move into sunshine and I'd be squinting against the glare on the ripples and thinking about taking off my sweatshirt.

I tore open the twelve-pack, dumped it into the tub, and began pouring the sack of cracked ice over it.

"Hey, kinda early, isn't it?" Ralph protested. He's a great protester.

"It'll be good and cold by the time we want it," I said. "You want any more coffee? I brought a thermos." I'm the new guy in this boat. Noonin advertised for a partner a couple of years ago when his last partner left town. I answered because Nancy had been complaining we never saw anybody but law enforcement people. I thought maybe she'd get together with the other boaters' wives and do girl stuff while we fished, and maybe meet us for picnics later, with jolly red-checked napkins in straw hampers. I'm good at creating pleasant images like that. But Ralph's wife always visits her family when he goes fishing, and the other guy we sometimes asked along wasn't married. In the end my wife came to resent the boat almost as much as the department. One good thing, there was no argument about who kept my share of the boat when we split.

Getting to be partners in a boat with Ralph was a good deal for me; he's an experienced fisherman. He landed a ten-pound walleye last year and got it mounted for the wall of his family room. Actually that's all you *can* do with a walleye that size; you wouldn't dare eat it. The headwaters of the Mississippi rise above the Twin Cities, and by the time that water gets down to the southeastern corner where we are, it's full of PCBs and other bad initials like that. Big fish that grow up in the Mississippi are good for trophies or for throwing back, take your pick.

"I always forget," I asked Ralph, "what's a PCB, anyway?"

"Uh ... polychlorinated biphenyl. But don't ask me what that means. All I know, you eat too many of them, you glow in the dark, and after that you get cancer." He poured the last of the coffee out of the thermos and nudged the boat a little closer to shore. "What made you bring that up? You in a bad mood or something?"

"Nah—I was just thinking about that trophy walleye you got last year."

Ralph beamed all over his smooth, round pink face. "Wasn't he a hummer though? Came up outta the water that first time like he was fired out of a *gun*, man—" We went back over the whole story then, replayed the entire catch from the first tug on the line to the weight of him in the net as he came into the boat.

Ralph likes to fish with me because I rarely catch my limit, so he can keep on fishing when he'd otherwise have to quit. He always offers to divvy the catch even with me. He doesn't mind sharing the catch, it's the fishing he likes. Sometimes I accept his generosity, sometimes I don't. The truth is I don't really give much of a rip if I never go home with a fish. I just like the time on the river, the little quick glimpses of birds and critters along the bank, the easy way we talk or don't talk after we've been out a while. I love the taste of very cold beer with the big salty sandwiches we always bring along, and the sound of the voices that come across the water from other boats, lazy and aimless, as if we'd all suddenly passed a law against hurrying.

By three-thirty we had eight or nine fish in the live well

and had worked our way back to the west side of the lake. I was lying in the stern half asleep, staring into the glint of sun on still water. I yawned contentedly, not thinking about anything. Then the big chasm in my face somehow opened a space in my brain, and a simple insight moved in and occupied it.

She had bored me. Nancy. My wife. She had never had anything to say that I wanted to hear. She was a dedicated channel-surfer, read *People* magazine with close attention and could quote from the pop psychology and celebrity gossip she picked up in the shop where she got her long nails glued on.

I met her on the dance floor, and from the moment I saw her, I wanted to get her into bed. The fun of dancing and the joy of pursuit carried me through the dating phase, and before long we were engaged and moved in together, or was it the other way around? And from then on we were planning a wedding, and Nancy was the resident expert on that subject. This part isn't interesting to guys, I thought, but later will be better.

She was pretty; it was fun introducing her as my wife. And without any doubt, her mainstream ancestry—her middle-class German-English-Irish bloodlines and unmistakable whiteness—was part of the thrill for me. She diluted the impact of my murky beginnings. Our children, I remember thinking happily, would know for sure what fifty percent of them was, and my love would make up to them for the uncertainty about my half.

Augmenting that was our mutual heat for each other; our first two years together passed in a blaze of delirious sexual passion. When they were over, except for yard work, I rarely found anything at home to amuse me. Sometimes, when she started rattling on about caring relationships and crystals and Christ knows what-all else, I used to curl my toes inside my shoes and grip the arms of my chair. Pretty soon I'd make a couple of phone calls and be out of there.

I had a dozen reasons, at the time, for staying away. Work was the best excuse, and due to the unstinting effort I gave it, I earned two promotions in five years of marriage. Then I decided to learn handball, and after that there was fishing. When she started giving me grief for never being home, I used her nagging as an excuse to stay away even more.

I had a big stake in the stability of my marriage; the foster child in me wanted to be a householder, a husband, and a father. That was the good life, right? When it turned out I couldn't stand the good life I got, I turned into an artful dodger. In retrospect, I think I should be forgiven for some of the lies I told Nancy; I told bigger whoppers to myself.

Even getting a divorce didn't make me come clean. All this past winter I had been moping and mourning because my wife had left me for another man. I got hurt and distressed every time I saw a couple shopping for groceries together, or cleaning out the garage. All the things I hadn't wanted to do with Nancy seemed desirable and sweet when I saw another man doing them with his wife. If only my wife hadn't started playing around, I told myself, I could be enjoying domesticity right now, instead of roosting in this scuzzy apartment eating take-out pizza alone.

Poor Nancy. No wonder she got so angry. I really left her first, but because I wouldn't admit there was anything wrong but her attitude, I still managed to blame her for cheating on me when she got a boyfriend. Pretty slick work, actually. I probably belonged in politics.

"Are you all right?" Noonin asked. "You got a bellyache or something?"

"No," I said, "Why?" He was staring at me in alarm. I was sitting bolt upright, gripping the sides of the boat.

"Just think we oughta get going, is all," I muttered. "Getting late."

"Sheee. Thought you must be havin' a coronary. Switch seats with me then, I'll get the motor going." Noons always acts as if I'm too incompetent to be trusted with an outboard, which I claim is the worst kind of a canard. Outboards are too unreliable to be trusted with my mental health.

We took our place in the homebound string of cars and boats. Ralph slid a couple of tapes of Hootie and the Blowfish into the deck, and we yelled at each other above the din. I don't know whether Ralph and I play loud music because our conversations are painfully inane, or the reverse. We've never tried silence in the car, so there's no way to be sure. Two or three rambling commentaries on the talents and salaries of various pro sports figures, plus a weather prediction and a tentative agreement to fish again the Sunday after next, took us halfway home, and from then on we were mostly silent.

It's restful, a long drive like that with a guy like Noonin. You know he's never going to use the word "beige" as long as "tan" is still in the dictionary. He has no desire to share details of his personal life with me, and he has no politics beyond bitching about taxes. I'm kind of free to let my mind wander.

Seeing the truth about Nancy and me seemed to have freed up a whole lot of synapses that were now firing at warp speed. As we rolled past fat blue silos standing by red barns in the glow of the late-afternoon sun, the events of the past week scrolled past me like a movie. By the time Noonin's station wagon topped the last rise above Rutherford, questions had begun circling my head like bees.

As soon as I was back in my own car, I headed for Jay Billingsley's shop. Jay peered out through the slats of his venetian blinds as soon as I knocked; he wore a curiously exalted expression as he let me in.

"Thought you'd be looking worn out and mean," I said as he handed me my two packs of prints and Mrs. LaPlante's yearbook.

"I'm dead," he said, beaming all over his skinny geek's face, "but—you want to see what I've got to show for it?"

He led me into his inner sanctum, where four dozen pictures were propped on drying racks around the room. They were exquisite prints of mating and nesting ducks, so sensual and intimate they raised my heartbeat.

"Holy cow," I said. "Jay. You're making me blush."

"I'm pretty excited," he said. "A couple of these are good enough for Sierra Club or the *National Geographic,* I think." He turned off the light. "I'm gonna go eat gross amounts of Chinese food and then sleep for ten hours. I hope I've seen the last of you for a while, for Pete's sake. What are we trying to do here, imitate Chicago?"

"Yup," I said, "nobody can say we're too slow to learn."

I'd intended to take the pictures home with me for the night, but now I found myself drawn toward the word processor in my office. It wouldn't hurt to stop in for just a minute, I decided, to type a few notes while the ideas were still fresh.

I was hunched over my screen an hour later when Frank poked his head in the door and said, "Hell's the matter with you, Jake, don't you have a home?"

"I'm writing down some questions to ruin your Monday with," I said. "Why are you down here now?"

"Russ Swenson's dad had a heart attack this afternoon. Russ called me and asked to get off. Usually I can put Schultzy or Mary Donovan into a spot like that, but they were both out of town today so I told him I'd take it for a while, and then I got Cunningham to come back for a while, and Ed Gray's gonna come on a couple hours early." He stretched and flopped into a chair. "What kinda questions? I'm gonna be in meetings most of the day tomorrow, can this wait till Tuesday, or you wanna tell me about it now?"

"Oh, no, Frank, listen, you need to get home and—" He shook his head impatiently.

"The three big kids have things on with friends today," he said, "and Sheila took Moira and Dan to see her mother. I'm not in a hurry. I'd like to hear what you got there, what's so important you came in here in your fishing britches to write it down."

"How'd you know I went fishing?"

"You kidding? Smell you all the way out in the hall. You do any good?"

"Five nice walleyes and a couple of saugers." Frank didn't need to know Noonin caught all but one. "Okay, you sure you're up for this?" I read my first question off my screen: "Why did Dornoch bury the clothes?"

"Whaddaya mean, why'd he bury them? To hide them, naturally."

"Okay, if that's true, here's number two: Why didn't he bury the hand? Why leave it in the freezer for us to find?"

"Well, because, you said before, he was saving it for—" He sat and stared at me for a minute and then said, "Oh."

"Precisely. What happened to the third victim he was saving it for? Why'd Dornoch lose interest? Why didn't we find a third man all dressed up in that softball gear we found in the garage?"

"He killed himself first."

"But why? All along I've been telling you, this man has a precise plan, this killer is very well organized, he knows just what he wants to do. That's the one thing about the crimes that does seem to fit Andy Dornoch, actually. Doesn't it? A neat, systematic, reliable man. Now, if a guy like that sets out to kill three people, he's gonna kill three people. So why did he suddenly stop after he'd killed two, and hang himself instead?"

"Remorse," Frank said.

"Bullshit. The man who killed Wahler and LaPlante wasn't feeling any remorse. Everything in those Polaroid pictures said, plain as day, Gotcha! That's why they worried you so much. Besides, if he was feeling remorse, why would he bury the clothes, why not leave them for us to find, make it all easy?"

"Well, come on now, is it too much to believe that he was going along killing guys, enjoying keeping us guessing the way they say these freaked-out killers do, and then for some reason on Saturday morning he sort of . . . came to, and said, 'Oh, what have I done?' and just decided to kill himself?"

"And left his gardening gear in the yard, and his car parked in the driveway with the keys in it, and his front door unlocked? Does that sound like the Andy Dornoch you knew?"

Frank shifted in his seat. "Well, no. I gotta admit, that's one part of this thing that's been bothering me, too. I can't imagine Andy ever leaving his tools out, even if hell was freezing over. Shit, though, Jake"—Frank threw his arms in the air impatiently—"aren't we trying to make sense out of something that we can't ever really understand? I mean, the guy just went around the bend—"

"Why?"

"Oh, now, wait a minute, Jake, that's not on my job description, figuring why some people go to La-la Land and some don't—"

"I know," I said, "but I thought about Dornoch all the way back from the river, remembering all the times I've seen him in the years since his daughter died, and what strikes me is, he may not have been deliriously happy, but he was doing his job, getting his snow shoveled and his zucchini picked. So why, after years of slogging along the way most of us do, plenty of shit eating on him but he's got his job to do and he does it, why all of a sudden does he start to cut up guys in the park and take their pictures? And how—"

"Nah, nah, nah," Frank stood up and shook his head vigorously. "You're getting way out in left field, now, Jake, this deep psychological junk won't get us anyplace. Just do the police work and follow where the evidence takes you. Listen, I gotta go—"

"You didn't let me finish," I said. "The rest of the question is, how, on the day he impulsively decides, To hell with a life of crime, I think I'll just hang myself on this nice handy tree instead, does he manage to jump off the ladder and strangle himself *first*, and *then* pull himself up over the tree limb and fasten the knot?"

Frank turned in the doorway. "*What?*"

"Or if that isn't what he did, how come the fresh bark that the rope pulled off the tree is all sticking out on the side away from the body?" I slid the envelope of pictures across the desk toward him. "Top photo," I said, "take a look."

He looked. He adjusted the light, dug out his reading glasses, and looked again. He turned the photo over as if the answer might be printed on the reverse side, then turned it back and studied it some more. Then he went back over to his chair, sat down, and said, "I'll be a sonofabitch." He chewed on it by himself a while and then asked me, "If you saw this Saturday, why didn't you tell me about it then?"

"Because I didn't see it Saturday. Remember how crazy it was in that yard by the time I took these pictures? I just aimed the camera and pushed the button. That's what I love about photographs, Frank, even these dogs I take, they almost always show you something you weren't quick enough to see at the site. I looked at these tonight, and there it was."

"Where's that rope now, by the way? Did they take it along with the body?"

"Yes. Well, the front part, with the knot in it. They cut him down, remember? And Pokey made an issue out of making sure they took the noose along so he could match up the rope and the bruises."

"But the rest of the rope got left on the tree? I know I should remember, but—"

"But you were doing about a hundred other things at the time. Yeah. Last I saw of it, the rest of the rope was still hanging over the limb, with the bottom end tied around the tree."

"Do you suppose—is it dark yet?" He peered out my blinds. "Not quite. Well, you've got your Streamlight in the car, anyway, haven't you? You wanna run over there and see if that rope is still there?"

"Okay," I said, "You gonna follow me, or—?"

"No, lemme ride with you. I had Sheila drop me off, we were at the St. Stephen's raffle when they paged me about Russ. I was gonna have one of the squads run me home."

"Have we still got a watch on the house?" I asked him, as we headed out toward Eighteenth Avenue.

"I don't have enough squads on a Sunday, to assign one full-time to Dornoch's house," he said. "I put a crime scene lock on the front and back doors and added it to the drive-by list for whatever cars were patrolling section eight."

"Who's got the duty tonight?"

"Um, Miller and Nguyen, I guess." We parked in front of Dornoch's house. I handed Frank my Streamlight, got out my camera, and started digging through the boxes in the backseat for some fresh film. A blue-and-white pulled in behind us and turned its brights on. Frank said, pleased, "Well, that was quick work," and stepped over to tell Les what we were doing. By the time I had my camera loaded they were getting out of the car.

"Les says he'd like to have Amy see how little bits of evidence can make a difference," Frank said, coming back. The four of us walked single file past the house in the lengthening shadows. It was even duskier in the backyard, but we could see the rope still hanging there. We stood under the tree, shining our lights up at the broken bits of bark protruding from the west side of the tree limb, the side away from where the body had been. It was plain enough, when you knew what to look for and were paying attention. The rope had been pulled across the limb in the wrong direction. We shone our lights on the grass and found broken bits of bark lying there, on the west side of the limb. The force of the line, with its heavy burden, had thrown some of them a couple of feet.

They all stood back while I took pictures.

"Nuts, I forgot, I'm all out of evidence bags in my car," I said.

"I've got some," Les said. "What do you want, one for the rope and one for the pieces of bark?" He headed back out front to get them. Frank was carefully lifting the rope off the limb, telling Amy, "See, you want to be careful because the technicians at BCA can put these fibers under a microscope and determine whether the ones that went over the limb are pointing the wrong way. Also—" His gaze, directed upward at the rope, went past it to the rear of the house, and he said, "Now, wouldn't that frost you? I could have sworn I checked every window in that house yesterday, but now look there, that middle one on the second floor has sprung open a couple of inches. It's those darn counterweights in those old windows, if you don't have the lock set just right they'll gradually pull the window open."

"I'll get it," I said. "You got the key to the back door lock?"

"Here," he said, "it's the window at the end of the hall, I think. Or it could be the bathroom."

The kitchen door swung open quietly on well-oiled hinges. I crossed the shiny tile floor, keeping my eyes away from the refrigerator. The pantry doors swung both ways, I remembered. Then I was in the dining room, with dishes and glassware glinting through the glass doors of a buffet. I padded across wall-to-wall carpeting to the hall, where my footsteps on the hardwood floor suddenly sounded so loud they startled me.

The Dornochs had carpeted the dining room and living room in a soft gray-green plush but left the hardwood floor of the hall bare, with a dark red Persian area rug near the front door. So pretty, I thought; the way the polished oak floor matched the wainscoting in the hall and welcomed you into the warm, old-fashioned house. The stairs were built of matching wood but had a wide strip of the same thick carpet that covered the dining room. I padded silently upward into the gloom. The grandfather clock I'd heard yesterday ticked on the landing. At the top of the stairs, I could dimly see that another strip of carpet led straight ahead down the hall, and that bedroom doors stood open on either side.

Why am I groping around in the dark here? I thought suddenly. The power's not off in this house. I groped for a switch and flooded the hall with light. Now I could see that the window at the end of the hall was firmly closed. I checked it anyway; it was locked down tight.

Two closed doors faced each other at the end of the hall. The one on my right was a small bathroom, with one small window over the sink, closed and locked. On the other side of the hall was a little sewing room, with many cupboards. It held spare furniture, a worktable, and a double closet with floor-to-ceiling doors. The window, which faced the backyard, was open a few inches above the sill. Crossing the room, I noticed one door of the closet slightly ajar and swung my left arm out absently to close it.

The door swung violently back, hitting the end of my middle finger so hard I heard the bone crack. I screamed at the top of my lungs. Somebody lunged out of the closet and knocked me down, going flat out for the door.

My right hand found something that moved, a stool or a small chair. From the floor, I threw it had hard as I could at the figure running away. It thudded into his back, driving him forward so he smacked into the door across the hall. He turned, blood streaming down the front of his face, his right hand groping at his back. I had my feet under me and was getting up, but the right hand came away from his back, holding a gun that must have been jammed in his belt there, and as I pushed up and forward I saw I was going to be too slow getting out of the way.

Then cause and effect seemed to come unglued. I heard the double roar as the big gun fired two shots, but I never felt a bullet hit me. The momentum of my lunge carried me crashing into the stacked furniture in the corner behind the open door. A lot of shouting followed, and the hall seemed to explode. Wedged behind a broken table, I flailed at a tangle of chair legs poking into me. My left hand was trapped under my body. It hurt so much I was going to throw up. Then Frank flew in through the door, yelling, "Jake?"

He began digging me out, shouting, "You all right? You shot or what?"

"I don't know," I said. He threw most of the chairs off me, and I pulled myself up. "My hand—" I held out my left hand. The middle finger stuck up at an odd angle. It hurt me desperately, but no blood was running out of it. "It doesn't seem to be shot, though," I said, wonderingly. I patted myself here and there, tentatively, with my right hand. "I don't think I got shot at all, Frank."

Which was true. I hadn't. Because Amy Nguyen, easily outdistancing the other two police officers to the top of the stairs, had braced her two small arms to textbook rigidity and put a clean shot through Harley Mundt's left shoulder.

· TWELVE ·

FRANK WAS RIGHT; THE REST WAS ROUTINE POLICE WORK. Pokey and the other docs, in the course of Monday morning's autopsy, found that Andy Dornoch had a broken larynx and massive bruises on his upper body, indicating he died in a choke-hold.

Jimmy Chang did brilliant work with the rope; he proved the fibers above the limb of the tree were crushed back toward the body, because it was hauled across the limb with the body already in it and then tied.

He found hair from all three crimes scenes that matched and then matched it to hair still on Dornoch's body. That placed Dornoch at the first two crimes. And Jimmy's DNA studies showed conclusively that the penis out of LaPlante's mouth came off Wahler's body.

Harley Mundt had already explained Crazy Week to me,

of course. We were doing all this work to prove what we already knew, that Dornoch had killed the first two men and Mundt had killed Dornoch. Because Frank said, "Confessions aren't worth shit after perps get a lawyer. Prove it."

Frank gave me all the help I needed for a thorough search of Dornoch's house. It took two days. Al Stearns found the picture we were looking for, inside a long-overdue library book from Hillside High School that was under the socks in Dornoch's bureau.

"Here," Stearns said, handing it to me with his face turned aside, looking as if he thought one pair of plastic gloves probably wasn't enough to protect him from the contamination of touching it.

It was an old Polaroid shot of Amanda Dornoch, naked, having sex with three young men. Wahler and LaPlante were in, or mostly in, their softball uniforms, and smiling broadly. Wahler's penis was in Amanda's vagina; LaPlante's was in her mouth. The picture had obviously been taken by a third male, using his left hand. His face and body were outside the picture frame, but his right arm, in the sleeve of a softball uniform, extended across Mandy's body from the lower edge of the photo. With his right hand, he was jacking off on her belly.

"Good work, Al," I said, trying to make it sound as if we'd just finished a roadside cleanup and were about to be awarded two tickets for the turkey raffle. Stearns looked as if he might get sick on me. I put the picture in a paper evidence bag. "We can wind this up now, I guess," I said to the rest of the search party. We were not a jolly group. Cops hate the shit that rolls over them when other cops commit a crime, and everybody in the department knew that Harley

Mundt was sitting in cell forty-three at the Hampstead County Jail.

"I knew he'd figured it out," Mundt told me. He stared blindly into the corner of the interrogation room, where I went every day during the week after he got out of the hospital after surgery. I had the middle finger of my left hand bandaged into a plastic cast; it still hurt some at night, and I had pills for the pain. Harley was wearing an upper-body cast and had his arm in a sling. Amy's bullet had passed through his upper arm, penetrated his chest cavity, nicked the bottom of his collarbone in front, and shattered the scapula, the large shoulder bone behind.

Harley was cooperative at first, waiving his right to an attorney and seemingly glad of a chance to tell somebody all about his terrible secret. We drank gallons of coffee together, more sociable, suddenly, then we'd ever been in the two years since he joined the department. I got to know him well, a truly discouraging experience.

"Mandy really belonged to the top clique." He pronounced it "click." "The kids who ran everything," Mundt said. "She thought she was kinda—oh, y'know, better than most of us, because her parents had a nice house and they gave her everything, pretty clothes and trips in the summer. She was always bragging about where she'd been, and that. But came party time, she wanted to be one of the fast ones. Liked to get down. Then she'd get friendly with the rowdy bunch, guys like Frenchy and Jim and me.

"It was after a ball game senior year, a bunch of us had a kegger, and we got a couple bottles of vodka, too. We really got blitzed, all of us. Mandy was even drunker than the rest of us, she'd been on some kind of a crazy grapefruit and cottage cheese diet all week, and the booze really went to her head. She seemed like she was ready for anything. So Jim rented a motel room, and we all went in it together, and—" He shifted in his chair. His glance slid past me and back to the corner.

"We didn't rape her. I know her dad wanted to believe we did, but she went willingly. She mighta done a bunch of stuff she wouldn't have if she was sober, but we didn't pour the stuff down her throat, either.

"But then afterward, the next week? She acted like we were dirt. Like, she kind of realized it got outta hand, so she turned over a new leaf. She started hanging with the kids that pulled grades and sucked up to teachers and stuff. Frenchy and me went up to her before the next game and said, 'Hey, Mandy, wanna come party with us after?' And she wouldn't even *talk* to us.

"So I had these pictures that I took that night, I don't think she even remembered me taking 'em. I told the guys, I said, watch how I make this bitch behave. I waited till study hall, and I found her in the library. I laid one of my pictures right across the top of the page she was reading, and I whispered in her ear how from now on, she better be nice to me, or maybe I'd just deliver one of these to her old man.

"She slammed the book shut on the picture and got up and left. She had an unexcused absence from the next class, and the next day they said she was home sick. I phoned her two or three times, trying to get her to come out of the house, but her mom wouldn't call her to the phone, she said she was sick.

"One of her friends, not so long after that, told Frenchy and me and some of the guys, that Mandy Dornoch was suffering from depression. Frenchy said, 'What's she got to be depressed about, a great ass like that?' and we all laughed, but this girl went off in a huff.

"Mandy never did come back to school, though. We all went ahead and graduated, and later that summer Mandy died. She just laid up there in her room and starved, till she got so depressed she took pills, I guess." He shook his head. "Crazy broad."

We were both silent for some time. "Harley," I asked suddenly, "why did you go on to college if you didn't like school?"

He glared into his coffee. "Stupid rules we got in this state. You have to have two years of college to join the police force. I always knew I wanted to be a cop, I like the status and I like the benefits. Damn good retirement." He kicked a table leg and said angrily, "I guess that's all gone to hell, now, huh? And it's not my fault, none of it, I had to defend myself against that crazy old man." He brooded. After a minute, he shrugged and asked, "Why? What made you ask about school?"

"Just curious. How'd you even get into college if your grades were so bad?"

"My SATs weren't that bad. And my dad had a friend who knew the dean. They persuaded him to let me do summer tutoring and try one semester. Then I started balling a chick who was a real dog, but one of these brains that got straight As. She was real grateful for the attention, and she made freshman year a breeze for me." He chuckled.

"Well, and so you got through school and joined the department, and you figured this business with Mandy was all behind you, right?" I asked him.

He stared at me incredulously. "I never even thought of her again," he said. "Why should I? She was nothing to me, we never even dated, not really.

"But right away when we found Wahler, as soon as I saw the uniform and that picture and the way he had been cut, in my heart I knew who did it and why. That's why I threw up. But at the same time I couldn't believe anybody'd be so crazy.... It just seemed so *nuts*. So I kept trying to convince myself that maybe it was just a coincidence. Then we found Frenchy, and I knew, beyond any doubt, I was gonna have to kill that crazy bastard or he was going to cut me up and leave me in a park too." He shivered. "Boy, I had nightmares, thinking how he was going to arrange that hand on me just so, and then take that goddamn picture."

"I still don't understand," Frank said, when I reported this conversation to him, "why Dornoch was okay with this for five years and then started killing the guys in the picture."

"He never saw the picture till now. His brother Steve explained that for me. He said, 'I've been worried about him for weeks, ever since he put Loretta in the hospital this last time. There was something about papers—he was trying to do some kind of long-term commitment, and he needed to find her birth certificate. He spent a long time going through all the papers in the house and . . . he never told me, specifically, about that picture,' Steve said, 'but the next time we talked he said he'd found the explanation for what happened to Amanda. And ever since then, he hasn't been a bit like himself, just very vague and distracted. At first I thought it was natural, his daughter gone and then having to put his wife away like that. But he didn't seem to snap out of it the way he always could before.' "

"Poor bastard," Frank said. "Okay, so—and the gear and uniforms were old stuff that accumulated in his lost-and-found over the years, I suppose."

"Right. The uniforms were from a City League team that was all put together a few years ago, and then lost its sponsor at the last minute. That's why they matched and were all unmarked. Dornoch had been doling them out as mid-season replacements. Grieve remembered them."

"Uh-huh. Well, what else, from all those questions you kept throwing at me? Oh, have you figured out yet why the gate was open, that first night?"

"Pretty sure. After I thought about it. He told me himself, the next morning. The first groups scheduled to use Pioneer Park Tuesday morning were Head Start. Dornoch wanted to be sure those little kids wouldn't be the ones to find the body. He left the gate ajar so the cops would find it first. See, he knew how often the park was patrolled at night. That's why all of this worked so well for him, because he knew the system for all the city facilities, inside and out."

Frank stared out the window a minute. "How do you suppose he figured out the third man was Mundt?" he said. "I'd never have known, from that picture."

"Who says he did? I mean, Mundt thinks he did, that's why Mundt killed him. And that's why he went back into the house to look for the picture. You didn't forget to lock that window, by the way. Harley climbed the drainpipe and jimmied the lock through the frame. He was absolutely convinced, and he still thinks, that if we'd found that picture we'd have known he was the third man, and that he was the one who killed Dornoch. But that's Mundt's guilt talking.

"He got obsessed with the idea of Dornoch coming after him, just the way Dornoch intended him to. That's what the Polaroid pictures on the bodies were for, Frank. Dornoch arranged those bodies the way he did, each one punished for precisely what he did to Amanda, and then took the picture and put it there, to send a message to the third man, 'This is what's in store for you.'

"It must have been driving Andy Dornoch out of his tree, the way you kept any news of the pictures out of the paper and off TV. Dornoch phoned in the anonymous tip, Frank, I'm sure of that. He was getting desperate by Friday night, because he'd killed both the men he knew about, and he figured he had to get the description of the pictures out there so the third man would show himself. It's so ironic. Because the one thing he didn't have to worry about was the third man getting the message. Harley was right here in the department, he knew all about the pictures. And Harley took the bait just the way Andy hoped he would."

"That's what the whole crazy business with the uniforms and pictures was all about, then? Dornoch was trying to get the third guy to come after him like that?"

"Yup."

"Jeez, you suppose it never occurred to him he could get killed himself? Or maybe he didn't care by then."

"Dornoch had stalked two men in the dark and strangled them from behind with a cable, and he was sure he'd be quicker than the third man, too, if he could just get him to show his face. Remember, we don't know that much about Andy Dornoch's Vietnam experiences. He may have had more practice killing guys in the dark than any of us gave him credit for. But Harley Mundt, as I humbly admit"—I held up my finger cast—"is fast and strong and dangerous."

"Tell me about it. How the hell did he get through all our screening tests? Makes me mad every time I think about it, guy like that in the department."

"You're going to have to think like the rest of the guys in the department, Frank," I said. "They're already saying, 'He may have worn the uniform, but he wasn't really a cop.'

"Besides, what test should have caught this? It's off the charts, isn't it? You'll never devise a system that will predict everything about human behavior. Mundt was doing all right till this came up. He might have gone his whole career and never done anything to apologize for."

"You think that? A killer? A guy who'd do what he did? I don't believe that." Frank thrashed around in his chair. "Bothers the hell out of me. Makes me feel like I don't know anything about judging character, after all these years. Shit! If you hadn't of yelled like that, he'd've killed you sure. That's the one thing I do feel good about," he said, beaming at me suddenly, "is that you remembered what I told you about yelling, all those years ago when I was training you."

I nodded brightly, smiling at him. I didn't have a clue what he was talking about.

"I used to teach it to all my trainees," he rambled on, sitting back in his groaning chair, enjoying himself for the first time in days. "I'm gonna remind all my FTOs to put it back into the routine training. It's one of those simple things that we get so damn clever and high-tech and forget about"—he swiveled noisily around and smiled fondly out the window—"that when you get in a tight spot and you can't get to your weapon, the best thing to do is holler your head off. Sometimes it'll scare off an attacker. Sometimes, like it did for you at Dornoch's house, it'll get you some help. And you remembered it in a very tight spot, that's what I feel so good about."

It didn't seem like the right time to tell McCafferty that I just yelled like that because Harley Mundt scared the piss out of me.

Trudy Hanson was impressed when she heard how my snapshots of broken bark made a difference in the case. She inspected them carefully and offered several pointers about how I could improve my camera technique, insider stuff like, "Try not to cut off the bottom of the object you're aiming at." I absorbed as much advice as I could at the time, but I pointed out that we were pretty busy with Dornoch's autopsy. I asked her if she'd be willing to show me some more neat tricks if I came up to St. Paul.

"Well . . . sure," she said, looking at me uncertainly. "You mean come to the lab some morning and—"

"Not exactly," I said, "I was thinking more like go out for dinner and dancing some night. And compare f-stops and stuff."

She flashed a million-megawatt grin that almost made me pass out. "Why, Jake!" she said, "You *fox!*"

We agreed on Friday. I took the afternoon off, got a haircut and a shoeshine and bought a new jacket, and was on her doorstep at seven o'clock precisely. That took some restraint, because I had been waiting around the corner since six-thirty-five.

She had her hair up in some kind of a wonderful do, in

curls on top with little tendrils hanging down. She was wearing a blue dress that matched her eyes. It was demurely cut, not particularly short or revealing, but it fit her in a subtle, clingy way that managed to look both elegant and titillating. I had used the drive to the Cities to debate the relative merits of a quiet little dinner versus a big night out. As soon as I saw Trudy Hanson's dress, I discarded all thought of quiet corner booths and uncorked Plan A.

"I've been working too hard," I said. "Let's do the towns and get giddy." I told her I wanted to see as much of the Twin Cities as she could cram into one evening, eating and drinking whatever wonderful stuff we found as we went along.

"Sort of grazing, you mean?" she asked, and I said, "Exactly! How quick you are. Let's graze."

We started with oysters and champagne in a waterside place on the Mississippi Mile, where a Valkyrie-sized blond woman played show tunes on a piano by the window. We touched glasses and made a pact not to discuss law enforcement for the entire evening. I said I wanted to hear more about nonteam sports, so she told me about taking a winter off during school to work as a waitress and be a ski bum in Colorado, and summers of resort work in Idaho and Montana, where she tried white-water rafting and rock climbing.

"You kind of like risks, huh?" I asked.

"Not really. I like developing skills, seeing how far I can go with something. It's a personal thing; I'm not interested in winning or losing."

"So—where do you draw the line in this thrill-seeking?"

She shrugged. "Wherever I get scared," she said, and smiled. It was fun talking to her; she never seemed to have any urgent need to make a point. You could agree with her, nor not, without rocking her boat at all.

After the oysters we walked along the river while the lights came on and turned the water into a long Christmas tree. I offered her my jacket, but she had a silky shawl that scrolled magically out of her bag. We strolled and talked trivia, books and movies mostly, and in a few minutes she said, "There's a place up in Edina that makes Caesar salad to die for, you up for that?"

We drove through many blocks of handsome real estate, stopping at last in front of a three-story house with many balconies. Inside, there was very faint piano music, candles, and a lot of stained glass.

"Are we going to eat or say mass?" I asked her. Then a handsome young man wheeled up a cartful of gleaming carafes and performed a sort of hand ballet. Lettuce, anchovies, and an egg appeared; magic potions dripped out of glass jugs. Eventually he laid two plates of glamorous-smelling romaine in front of us, smiled benignly, and wheeled away.

"I was almost right," I said, "it's some kind of cult thing, isn't it?"

"Bet you don't make any more jokes after you taste it," Trudy said. After one cautious forkful, I shut up and snarfed it down to the last crouton.

"That was wonderful," I said as we left. "You're good at this guiding stuff."

"Glad you're pleased," she said, "but the best is still to come. Wait, now, I have to use a map for this." She directed me to the old part of St. Paul, where we negotiated several narrow alleys to the doorway of a nondescript-looking Italian restaurant where old guys in felt slippers sat on bentwood chairs, contentedly insulting each other. We split a cannoli so good it almost made me cry.

"Now, Jake, be honest," Trudy said, as we carried all those calories onto the sidewalk, "aren't you getting tired? Because after all you had surgery on that hand just a few days ago—"

"On the contrary," I said, "I'm starting to get happy feet. Isn't there a dancing portion on this tour?"

She treated me to one of her zillion-megawatt grins then and crowed, "Oh, hot dog! You really do want to dance!"

We rolled down the windows and breathed alternating drafts of gasoline fumes and spring flowers on the long drive back across the river. Rolling along in the alternating bright-dark-bright of street illumination, she told me some more hair-raising stories about climbing in the Rockies. Then I described some of my dumber fishing mistakes, so I could watch her laugh. I was so happy watching gleaming white teeth and dimples I was almost sorry when she pointed the way to a dance club in south Minneapolis. It was a jazz cellar with a dance floor so crowded it would have been condemned for any other purpose, where we danced like mad things until the band refused any more encores and began packing their instruments.

While the stars grew pale above Fort Snelling, we chattered and giggled our way back to her place. At the door she said, "Want me to make you a cup of coffee before you start that long drive home?"

"That sounds great," I lied. I wasn't going to push her, though. I helped her get the cups out of the cupboard, and we got as far as running some water in the pot. Then she turned away from the sink suddenly, said, "Jake . . . ," and put her hand against my cheek. I kissed her till she made a little sound that said it all for both of us.

She took my hand. I followed her down a narrow hall to a small, fragrant bedroom. Like good children doing our chores, we opened the window, turned down the quilt, and helped each other undress. Standing close together then, while a bird outside her window made the first soft sounds of morning, together we let down her golden hair.